MELISSA DE LA CRUZ

DISNEY • HYPERION

Los Angeles   New York

First Edition, March 2021
10 9 8 7 6 5 4 3 2 1
FAC-020093-21015
Printed in the United States of America

This book is set in Adobe Caslon Pro
Designed by Torborg Davern
Library of Congress Cataloging-in-Publication Data
Names: De la Cruz, Melissa, 1971– author.
Title: High school musical the musical: the roadtrip / Melissa de la Cruz.
Description: First edition. • Los Angeles ; New York : Disney-Hyperion,
2021. • Audience: Ages 8–12. • Audience: Grades 7–9. • Summary: Just after
finishing a production of *High School Musical: The Musical*, a group of Utah
high school students goes to Jackson Hole, Wyoming, for a High School
Musical convention.
Identifiers: LCCN 2020038080 • ISBN 9781368061841 (hardcover) • ISBN
9781368062015 (ebook)
Subjects: CYAC: Musicals—Fiction. • Congresses and conventions—Fiction. •
Friendship—Fiction. • Dating (Social customs)—Fiction.
Classification: LCC PZ7.D36967 Hig 2021 • DDC [Fic]—dc23
LC record available at https://lccn.loc.gov/2020038080

Reinforced binding
Visit www.DisneyBooks.com

SUSTAINABLE FORESTRY INITIATIVE | Certified Sourcing
www.sfiprogram.org
SFI-00993

Logo Applies to Text Stock Only

For all the Wildcats—past, present, and future!

THE ROAD TRIP

CHAPTER ONE

CARLOS

Let me bring you up to speed.

High School Musical: The Musical—over. Huge success. HUGE. Kiss-and-cry backstage, then in the foyer with all our dumbstruck parents still waving their glitter signs and autographed programs, their hair crazy with Robotics Club confetti.

Cast-party time. Plan A is go crazy at Ashlyn's—part *deux*—but cast + crew + hangers-on = way too many people. Wouldn't want anything smashed, broken, or spilled. So Miss Jenn suggests we do what East High musical casts have always done: go to Denny's on West 500th and pretend it's a diner on the corner of Hollywood and Vine.

If we can make our school gym into a theater and a skateboarder into our star, then we can turn a Denny's in

Salt Lake City into Radio City Music Hall—especially when E.J.'s father is paying for all the milkshakes and onion rings.

We're all there (in this together, right?) screeching and singing and making Miss Jenn do her *Is that the last apple?* line again when my phone dings. It's not my sweet Seb, because he's holding court nearby—still in his Sharpay makeup—reprising his big number with the help of some built-in plastic seating and E.J.'s knee.

It's something much, much better. An *HSM* alert!

> Picked out the colors for your dressing room yet?

> One week till the HSM Convention in Jackson Hole!

What. The. Wildcats.

How did I miss this? I've been so consumed with our own show—choreography, drama, homecoming, Miss Jenn almost getting fired, the theater burning down, break-ups, make-ups, more drama, having to go on as a last-minute understudy and say things like *bro*—I haven't been paying attention to my *HSM* alerts. I didn't want to mess with the flow and now: Oh no!

"Miss Jenn." I grab her arm and she twirls so fast she takes out half the basketball team with her mermaid waves. "We have to do this."

She stares at my phone, her blue eyes wide.

"Next weekend?" she says, and pulls out her own phone. It has a green cover to remind her of when she was the understudy for Glinda in *Wicked*—I think it was in Peoria. Miss Jenn is pretty speedy with Google searches: You'd never guess she grew up in the old flip-phone days when people still used paper maps and never took pictures of their food.

"Panels," she says, scrolling with one pink fingernail. "Vocal workshops. Choreography workshops. Cosplay. And . . . oh! Oh!"

"What is it, Miss Jenn?" She looks like she's about to faint. That, or hyperventilate.

"Lucas Grabeel," she whispers. "Lucas Grabeel is going to be there, in person. Not a dream, Carlos. Actually in person!"

"Um, a dream?" I ask, and Miss Jenn whips her phone away.

"I have to go."

"Now?" There are more curly fries coming. Nobody leaves a party when curly fries are on the way.

"I mean, *we* have to go. To Jackson. Help me up." Miss Jenn elbows Seb off his perch and waves her hands to get everyone's attention. This doesn't work.

"Hey! Everyone! Quiet!" E.J. shouts in his best captain-of-everything voice, but that also doesn't work. Some of the chorus-line tap-dancing doesn't work, though it does bring the manager out to ask us to "Mind the floors, kids." And Gina leaping so high in the air she practically brushes the ceiling with her fingertips—no, that doesn't work either.

Finally Kourtney clambers up next to Miss Jenn and starts singing "I Can't Take My Eyes Off of You" at the top of her voice. Everyone's whooping and clapping and then Kourtney stops mid-line.

"Miss Jenn has something to say."

"Speech! Speech!"

"Not a speech," says Miss Jenn. I haven't seen her face this pale since the day the principal wanted to fire her. "An opportunity. You know how I always say to trust the process?"

More clapping and whooping. We have to shush everyone all over again.

"Well, sometimes you have to trust providence as well. You have to trust fate. You have to trust that the universe will provide."

"Has she got a Broadway callback or something?" Seb mutters in my ear.

"You're not leaving, Miss Jenn?" calls Nini. It's the first time she's taken her eyes off Ricky since we got here.

"Not leaving, Nini. Going. We're *all* going."

"To Disneyland?" asks Big Red, and everyone laughs.

"To Jackson Hole," Miss Jenn announces, and no one's laughing or whooping now.

"Skiing?" someone says, but no one looks too enthusiastic. They're all thinking about the curly fries, which are—let's face it—more exciting than Miss Jenn's announcement. She's selling it the wrong way.

"You guys, wait!" I shout. "It's a *High School Musical* convention—in Jackson Hole. Next weekend!"

Now everyone's talking. People are practically bouncing off the walls. I wish they'd put this amount of energy into their dance rehearsals.

"It would be the most amazing thing ever," Ashlyn says. "Meet-and-greets with some of the original cast and crew? Wow."

"But how would we get there?" Natalie asks. I hope she's not planning to bring her emotional-support hamster. The last thing we need is for that thing to escape in another state.

"Yeah," says Ashlyn. "I mean, E.J. can drive because he's *old*, but—"

"I can drive the school van," says Miss Jenn. "Mr. Mazzara gets it all the time for his robotics whatnots. I'll send permission slips to all your parents. I mean, they have to say yes. After seeing you all on the stage tonight—"

"Well, the gym," says Natalie. "Strictly speaking."

"It'll be a theater field trip," Miss Jenn continues. "A celebration of our amazing show. Research and nourishment for our creative souls."

She starts wobbling on her high heels with excitement, and Ricky helps her down from the chair. He's beaming so wide, his face almost splits in two.

"We have to make it happen," he tells her, and the dog tag around his neck glints in the fluorescent light. Since when does Ricky Bowen wear necklaces?

"Do you think Principal Gutierrez will agree?" Nini asks. Her face is still shining from the night's success. I mean, we *did* kill out there tonight. "Will we have to take time off school?"

"We really can't," Natalie tells Miss Jenn. "We have tests, and after school we have to rehearse every day."

Natalie's a killjoy, but she's right. We've promised to do a charity show on Christmas Eve to raise money; we have to help rebuild the school's burnt-out theater, after the fire that was (*whisper*) caused by Miss Jenn and Mr. Mazzara.

"And it will take us so long to get there," Natalie says.

"Five hours," E.J. reads from his phone. "That's the driving time. It's nothing. I've driven farther for archery lessons."

"Plus two hours when we get stuck in the snow," says Ashlyn. "You know, after the blizzard rolls in."

"We're driving a few hours north," I tell her, "not taking the Donner Pass."

"So we leave right after school next Friday," says Miss Jenn, eyes fixed on some distant spot, as though she's about to begin a power ballad. "And if we limit ourselves to one rest stop, we'll make it in time for some of the opening sessions that night."

"It ends on Saturday night," Kourtney says, scrolling down the site that practically every one of us is reading right now. "That's a shame. The final session is a group sing-along."

"We don't need to sing it," Ricky agrees, grinning at Nini. "We just lived it."

For someone who totally missed the boat on the

phenomenon that is *HSM*—i.e., did not grow up watching it with his mom, singing it in the car, and reenacting dance moves on the down-low in our high school cafeteria—Ricky is all about it now. I used to think his feet were glued to his skateboard. Maybe it's because being in the musical brought him and Nini back together, and he's already thinking about the spring musical and his next chance to stare into her eyes under the spotlight. He better watch out: E.J. may be over his selfless kick by then. Seniors in their last semester can get grabby with roles. They come over all sentimental about leaving school and this being their Last Chance Ever. Ricky should be on his guard. I mean, hasn't he seen *HSM3*?

Miss Jenn mutters something about going back to work right away to e-mail all our parents and break into the admin office to book the van. I hope she's joking about that last part. She's out the door before we can stop her.

"There's even a songwriting workshop," Ashlyn says to no one in particular, smiling at her phone. "I have to do that. I have to."

"I don't see any stage-makeup workshops," Kourtney says, and Nini mock-punches her.

"You need to go to one of the singing workshops," she tells Kourtney. "People need to hear your voice. You know what Miss Jenn told you—she said you were the best singer in Utah."

"*Northern* Utah." Kourtney rolls her eyes. "And she didn't say anything about southern Wyoming."

"Gina, you can come?" Nini says, and hugs her close. Things are way more chill between the girls these days. That's the magic of musicals, people! "You don't have to go back to DC right away, do you?"

Gina does some weird thing with her head that makes her look like one of those fake head-bobbing dogs in the back of old people's cars. She and Ashlyn exchange glances.

"Maybe," she says. "I hope so."

"Road trip!" shouts Big Red, and everyone starts leaping around and shouting again. At this rate they'll have no voices for the convention next weekend, whether they want to join the sing-along or not.

It's only then that I notice something strange. Seb hasn't said a word, and he's not looking at his phone.

"Can you go?" I ask him. Seb looks down at the floor.

"I don't know," he says. "It's a really busy time on the farm now. We have the last stock sale of the year on Saturday. It was a big deal for so many of my family members to come see the show tonight. I don't know if they can spare me that day."

Just like that, my excitement disappears. Not even an

HSM convention will be fun if Seb isn't there to hang out with.

"Hey," he says, and takes my hand. "Maybe something'll work out. Remember what Miss Jenn always says."

"'Trust the process'?"

"Nope." He shakes his head and smiles up at me. "'Is that the last apple?'"

We both laugh, but what I think is this: How can all these Cinderellas go to the ball? We've got to make some magic happen, people. This isn't a game. It's *High School Musical.*

Okay—it's *High School Musical: The Convention.* We're going to Wyoming, not a palace, and we need a van, not a pumpkin coach. A boy can dream, can't he?

Insta Interlude

E.J. here.

Now that it's the holiday season, I'm thinking about giving. We should all be more generous. It's never too soon to start giving. If we don't give, we don't get—and if we don't forgive, we don't forget. Isn't that right? At least, I think it is. Anyway.

I've been doing some forgiving and forgetting of my own. Not exactly living my best life right now. One minute I thought I'd found true love, and the next I was doing the right thing and stepping aside.

So for me it's also kind of a soul-searching time. Not that my soul is lost or anything. I just need some time to think. And to Insta my thinking, of course, so you all know what I'm thinking. No point in searching if you keep everything you're finding to yourself.

The thing is, next semester is my last at high school. Soon I'll be out in the real world, whatever

13

and wherever that is. High school's a cocoon, I guess, and you can get cozy in a cocoon. Before I hit the chill of someplace else, I need to think: Who am I, really? What's the best version of me?

It may seem weird, but the first stop on this journey for me has to be *High School Musical: The Musical: The Convention*, coming up super soon in a magical land just across the state line. I realize that this is the perfect place for me to review the past, live for the moment, and work out how to totally crush the future.

Stay tuned. Only good things can come of this. I'm convinced. Have you seen my smile?

E.J. out.

365 likes

Add a comment...

CHAPTER TWO

KOURTNEY

Now that the show's over, life can be normal again.

Who am I kidding? Nothing is normal anymore. The night after the show, Nini asks me to have a sleepover, and of course I say yes. That girl's house is my second home. Her moms are the best, and they always make me feel welcome. I love my own house, and my own parents, but my sweet spot is sitting in Nini's swinging basket chair, all curled up, talking about everything and nothing for hours.

Recently we've had way too much drama—and I'm not even talking about the show. That whole Nini-Ricky-E.J. love triangle got too much for my girl, and for a while she forgot who she really was: Nini Salazar-Roberts, a bundle of pure talent. Not Ricky's girlfriend. Not E.J.'s girlfriend. A rising star.

"So now that it's all back on with you and Ricky B," I say, stretching out one bare foot to examine my pedicure, "you have to promise me something."

Nini looks up from the ukulele, where she's picking out the tune of a new song.

"What?" she asks.

"Don't lose sight of you. That's all."

"You want me to look in the mirror more? Act like Sharpay?" Nini smiles at me and starts picking at the strings again.

"Say what you like about Sharpay." I tuck my foot back under the blanket. Outside the wind rattles the trees, and rain patters against the windows. The strings of lights above Nini's bed sparkle like stars. "That girl kept her eye on the prize."

Nini frowns at the fret and adjusts her grip. "She doesn't get the prize, though, does she? Ryan's the one who gets the place at Juilliard."

"Don't worry about Sharpay," I tell her. I can't believe we're talking about Sharpay and Ryan as though they're real people and not just characters in a movie. *Three* movies that we spent our childhoods watching over and over, but still. "She'll be fine, whatever she does. Just like you and me!"

Nini's quiet, and I wonder if she's thinking about her plans for next semester. I was the one who submitted an application on Nini's behalf to YAC—the Youth Actors Conservatory in Denver. Sometimes Nini loses her nerve, and I have to have enough nerve for the both of us. At the show she freaked out when she spotted the YAC dean in the audience: a lady with a clipboard, looking real stern. The lady left before the curtain calls. Super annoying.

"You know, that school in Denver might have been okay, but . . ."

"But what?" Nini stops playing. She looks stricken, like she ate way too much pizza.

I want to say something here about trusting the process, but I still don't really know what Miss Jenn is talking about half the time.

"Just that—you'll have a thousand other opportunities in your life. You are so talented, and such a good performer, and—"

"Kourt."

"No, really, you have to believe me. You're an amazing actress and—"

"*Kourtney*. I got in."

"What?" I almost fall out of the basket chair.

"The dean, Kalyani Patel. She talked to me after the show last night."

"But I thought she left? You *said* she'd left."

"I thought she had." Nini lays down the ukulele and stretches out on her bed, facing me. "But she'd just stepped out to call someone. She talked to me in the hall, just before we all left to go to Denny's."

"Why didn't you say something?" I can't believe she's kept this quiet for almost twenty-four hours. "There I was feeling sorry for you!"

"I apologize," Nini tells me. "Part of me can't believe it. And I haven't told anyone—not even my moms. You're the first person, and you have to promise me you won't say a word yet."

"Sure," I say, though I'm not sure at all. "Why the big secret? You really wanted this. Look how devastated you were when you thought she had gone."

"You're right. I was—devastated. But then I got distracted. Everything happened so fast. Ricky and I talked, and he told me he loved me."

"I know, I know." Anyone with eyes in their head last night could see that things with Ricky were back on. Even with everyone screeching like banshees at the party,

Nini managed to shout in my ear that Ricky had declared his love. About time.

But now I'm worried. Ricky loves Nini. Nini wants to go to YAC in Denver. But Nini loves Ricky. . . .

"Don't tell me you're going to turn down a place at an exclusive performing-arts conservatory and a launch pad to superstardom just because Ricky Bowen decides he loves you!"

"Of course not! I don't want to turn down YAC. I have to talk it all through with my moms, of course, but I think they'll be supportive. It's just—Ricky."

"And?" I give her my most feminist-fierce stare.

"I have to find the right time to tell him." She sits up, clutching at one of her old soft toys for comfort. She always goes for the lion, I can't help noticing; I have its twin on my own bed at home. We got them after our parents took us to see *The Lion King on Ice* when we were in sixth grade.

"You have to tell him soon," I say. "When are you supposed to start?"

"After the holidays."

"Wait—*these* holidays? Like, she wants you to start there next month?"

Nini nods. She looks as though she's about to cry.

"I'm scared," she tells me. "You won't be there. You've always been there."

"And I'll still be there for you no matter where you live," I say, though I feel scared and sad as well. We've been a team for so long.

"Ricky's always been there as well," she says. "He's spent this entire semester trying to win me back, and now I'm just throwing it all in his face."

"Nini, it's the twenty-first century. You're moving one state away. We have phones and computers. We have cars and planes. We have Instagram, if E.J. hasn't used it all up. And anyway, Ricky will understand what a big deal this is for you."

"But you know his mom just left. She's living in Chicago now, and she has a whole new life there. I don't know if he can take someone else leaving."

"He's still got Big Red," I reassure her. "And me. And Carlos. And Ashlyn. The whole theater gang!"

Rain lashes the windows and even though the room is cozy, we both shiver.

"I guess I'm not sure the best way to tell him," says Nini, wriggling under her comforter. "Or the best time. If we go to the convention next weekend, I don't want this to be some kind of dark cloud. It may be the last time we're all together for a while."

This gets me thinking. Plotting. Strategic thinking, I'd like to call it. "How about . . . ?" I begin, rocking the basket chair so it feels as though it's hanging from a wintry branch rather than a rafter. "How about you say nothing to Ricky until *after* the trip to the convention? That way you get to have tons of fun, spend a lot of time together, have a blast."

"You mean one last time. Kourt, I can't keep it from him for a whole week. I'll feel so guilty and weird."

"What's the alternative? You know how much he's looking forward to this. Who knew he'd turn into such a musical freak?" *Not me*, I want to say. *No way.* But then, I never imagined I'd get dragged into the show either.

Nini flops back on her pillows with a sigh that would make Sharpay proud. "So either I ruin the trip for him before, or ruin it afterward."

"Don't look at it that way. Your good news shouldn't ruin anything for him. He loves you, remember?"

Nini sits up like someone in a movie woken by a bad dream.

"You don't think I'm selfish wanting to study in Denver, do you?"

"No. Stop looking for excuses to . . . to Stick to the Status Quo!"

She throws the stuffed lion at me.

"Maybe," Nini says, "at the convention, I could do something like get him a special gift. You know, he's told me how *High School Musical* will always hold a special place in his heart because of how it helped us to get back together."

"Sweet!"

"So at the convention there are going to be original cast members, right? Maybe I can get them to sign a program or something, and give it to him as a memento of the show. To show him how important he is to me, and how special the show is to us both."

"If you get all those signatures, you're going to have to drag that program from Carlos's cold, dead hands. It'll be the greatest *HSM* souvenir of all time."

We both laugh, and Nini's phone decides to join in, buzzing away on the bed.

"Speak of the devil," she says, and then she's lost to me for the next ten minutes, texting back and forth with her very own Troy Bolton, smiling away at all the cute things he's saying.

So I snuggle back into the basket seat and close my eyes. I've always liked the sound of rain at night; it helps me clear my mind. Nini's not the only one considering new directions, new steps into the unknown. I've always been a backstage kind of gal, keeping my singing for church. But now Miss Jenn is telling me to step into the spotlight. Nini's trying to talk me into a singing workshop at the convention next week.

Maybe I could audition for the spring musical. Could I? I've never seen myself as an actor or performer, and we can all agree that while I've got moves, I'm no dancer. Am I just deluding myself by thinking I could take center stage? Chances are I wouldn't make it past the auditions. Miss Jenn and Carlos would take one look at me standing there, a blank look on my face—despite my amazing eye shadow—and send me backstage where I belong.

I decide not to say anything to Nini. She's got plenty to think about right now. I need to support her so she doesn't lose her nerve about this YAC opportunity. Now that the show's over, I need to come back down to earth.

A tree branch thwacks against the window and I almost jump out of my skin. Nini doesn't even seem to notice. She's gazing at Ricky's latest text, her face lit up with a smile. I want to hold on to this moment for as long as we can. In the new year she'll be moving to Denver, and we may not have the opportunity to hang like this for a long time.

I know we have to grow up and do things. But sometimes, deep down, I wish we could stay girls forever, with
our matching soft toys, and our dreams about the future
just that—dreams.

CHAPTER THREE

Miss Jenn's Top Eleven Rules
for Getting What She Wants
(i.e., the School Minivan and the
Trip to the *HSM* Convention)

1. Don't ask. Demand. Principal Gutierrez is a reasonable man, but this is no time for reason. Tell him you need the school minivan to drive to Jackson Hole on a trip of supreme cultural importance and educational significance. Try not to use the phrase *cosmic synergy*, however much it's dying to slip out of your mouth. Just make this sound serious and vital, like a visit to the Smithsonian, except with more singing and dancing.

2. Avoid Mr. Mazzara, who is sure to think of something robotics-related that's happening

the exact same weekend, because Mr. Mazzara and his robotics-related friends have no social lives and need to have quizzes or experiments or whatever it is they do every single Saturday. (Go to the mall already, Mazzara!)

3. Actually, Mazzara might be helpful. Remember when you had that "how to levitate Troy" problem in the musical, and he stepped right in and made it work? And then you watched *Big Hero 6* together and it was . . . nice. Well, until somehow the theater caught on fire. Okay, next point.

4. Jump on Mazzara when he waves at you in the staff room/flags you down in the hallway, and convince him to book the minivan for you. He owes you one for distributing those robotics stickers at opening night. That's only fair. And if all else fails—compliment him on those weird knitted neckties he wears. Yes, compliment him. Even though his grandma must make them for him, because it's inconceivable any store would sell them.

5. E-mail permission slips to all the parents and assure them that a) you are a trained van driver, b) you will be chaperoning everyone all the time and not having any fun yourself, c) everyone will only need one night of accommodation, and d) you'll deliver them all home before midnight on Saturday. Do not mention that LUCAS GRABEEL himself will be at the convention, and certainly do not type his name all in caps as though you're an obsessive fangirl rather than a Professional Teacher (or similar).

6. Google "how to become a trained van driver in the state of Utah."

7. Promise Principal Gutierrez that during this trip no one will get lost or go missing, no accidents will occur, no hearts will be broken, and no voices will be strained. Promise him that all the students who go to *High School Musical: The Musical: The Convention* will think of this as the best weekend of their lives, and later— when they are all wealthy and famous—will endow the school with scholarships and make

the school the most famous school in America, even more famous than the one in the movie *Fame*.

8. Pause to give Kourtney advice. She is such a good kid. When she asks what you meant when you said you have "big plans" for her, remember how blown away you were by her voice. Don't confuse *plans* with *vans* and get distracted imagining a fleet of supersize vehicles driving in convoy to Wyoming on Friday. When Kourtney tells you she is thinking about maybe auditioning for the spring musical, remind her that there is no *maybe* about it. So much talent! This is why you became a teacher. (Except you didn't really become a teacher, and almost got fired earlier this semester when everyone found out.)

9. Stay focused. Don't get distracted by thinking about that guy Mike you met at the bowling alley. That guy Mike is Ricky Bowen's dad. Is it too weird to date a student's father? Would that make you the evil stepmother? Does he own a backup minivan, just in case? Really, you have to stay focused.

10. Check the sign-up sheet. Call the hotel in Jackson Hole to reserve rooms. Discover the hotel is full and book rooms at a motel that's just outside town. Glance at the weather forecast for this weekend and ignore the symbol that looks like a snowflake. It's probably just some powdered sugar you sprinkled by accident on your phone. Walk to class singing *This van is my van / This van is our van / We'll drive it on Friday / To our convention* in case Mr. Mazzara is passing by and planning something sneaky.

11. Take a deep breath. This can happen. You are Miss Jenn, the designer of dreams, the dreamer of magic, the magician of music, the musician of design. . . . Okay. So you don't know where you're going with this. But you know where you *are* going? To the *High School Musical: The Musical: The Convention.* In Jackson Hole. This weekend. Even if you all have to walk there in the snow.*

*Not literally, of course, because you'll have that minivan, and the weather is sure to be fine.

CHAPTER FOUR

GINA

Other kids think I'm tough. Cold, unfriendly. When you've been to as many schools as I have, it's inevitable. That's just the way you have to be. Keep a hard shell to hide the mush inside. When you're the new girl carrying her tray across yet another strange cafeteria, everyone staring, no one wanting you to sit down with them, you have to be tough. I've learned the hard way that no one wants to make friends with you, or stay friends with you, when you're a transfer student who's only sticking around for a semester.

All of the above was true until I came to East High. We've had our growing pains, I know. My mom likes to call it a learning curve. She works for FEMA and has to move wherever the job takes her, so she's used to learning curves. It's not so easy when you're at an actual place of learning, like a school. Especially not when you can sing and dance, and get the big roles in school musicals.

Most of that drama set are juniors and I'm a sophomore, and at the beginning that added to my outsider status. When I first arrived at East High, I had gone to five schools in seven years. I needed to be confident, because that was my armor. If I was an outsider at every single one of these schools, at least I could be the star of the show. Before I went to school here, I used to tell myself, *If you don't care about people, you don't care what they think of you.*

But there's something about this place that feels different from all my other schools. These kids are genuinely friendly. They're good people. Sure, they bristled when I showed up at the auditions and danced them all off the stage. And we've had our ups and downs along the way, and maybe I did steal Nini's cell phone, and maybe I did try to dance-shame Nini, and change the rehearsal schedule, and cause maximum trouble by going to the homecoming dance with E.J.—but that's all ancient history now. Look at E.J.—he might have been furious with me. Instead he bought me a plane ticket so I could come back to Utah for the show.

This East High crowd is into forgiving and forgetting.

When they sing "We're All in This Together" they really mean it. Old Gina would have scoffed. But New Gina is kind of touched by it.

And now Ashlyn has made the most incredible offer. After she told her parents how I have to move cities *again* when I've just arrived, and just settled down, and just made friends, she tracked me down to ask if maybe I could stay with her family, to see out the school year.

I call my mom to tell her. I'm almost hyperventilating with excitement.

"It means no new school," I say. "No new trying-to-make-friends. I can stay here with the friends I've made and maybe get the lead in the spring musical."

"Gina, honey," my mom says, and I realize she doesn't sound excited at all. "Slow down a minute. You've been at East High for a few months. Sure, this sounds great now, when you've just been in a show, and you've all had fun together. But that's different from living with strangers."

"That's what I'm trying to tell you! They're not strangers. Not anymore."

"A few months," my mom says again. "You've been there a few months. You're in the honeymoon phase right now. Think about next semester, living with a family you don't know, when you have tests and homework and more stress. And say you get the lead in the musical, which I'm sure you will—because no one there could possibly have your talent and experience. Maybe they'll turn on you, these new friends of yours."

I don't reply. Mom isn't wrong, exactly. This has happened before, at other schools. Other kids seem to like me, and then when they decide I've "stolen" the lead from someone they've known since kindergarten, I'm out in the cold again. Mom is talking to someone in her office: I can hear the buzz of voices and maybe a photocopier. It's the weekend, but my mom works all the time. A crisis, she says, doesn't know one day of the week from the next. Kind of like the theater.

"Hon, I have to go," Mom says. "You're staying with Ashlyn's family this week."

"And going on the school trip on Friday," I remind her. There's no way I'm missing out on that.

"Yes, yes," she says, and I can tell she's already thinking about work again. "So just see how it goes. Then we can talk again once you're home."

"Okay," I agree, though I don't agree. Now is not the time to argue. When my mother is in work mode, she doesn't hear me at all. There's no point in saying that the new house in DC where our suitcases and boxes aren't even unpacked isn't "home" to me. I've spent more time in Ashlyn's house than our new place, or at least that's what it feels like. And there are even people around at dinnertime so I'm not eating alone, watching K-pop clips on YouTube. Ashlyn's mom wants me to run family stretch-and-strengthen sessions in their basement, though I think she's the only family member who's really into it. Everyone else claims to be allergic to incense.

The road trip is important, because I don't want Ashlyn to change her mind about letting me stay. Though Ashlyn is supercool and funny, I worry that we don't really have a lot in common. We're in different years at school, so at home we'll be studying by ourselves, working on different assignments. Maybe she'll get tired of having me around all the time at her house, taking up space in her room.

I'm going to do my best to be a supportive friend all weekend, and make sure Ashlyn has the best time. Nothing's going wrong on this trip, I promise.

Living in your own private Idaho? You're in the wrong state! Join us in WY this weekend for the HSM Convention!

What you've been looking for: vocal workshops for beginners/advanced. #HSMCon

Planning a sequel? Don't Scream! Hear our industry panel discussing staging HSM2!

The boys are back . . . and @ #HSMCon
Bop to the top of the line and our original cast members will SIGN!

Wanna feel fabulous? Try our "get loose" workshop for dancers of all abilities @ #HSMCon!

I can't take my eyes off of you . . . in the duets class! Learn how me + you = killer power ballads #HSMCon

CHAPTER FIVE

RICKY

After the show my mom went straight back to Chicago with her new boyfriend, Todd. We only had the chance to talk for a little while, but I felt a bit better about it. She seems happy, and she says my dad is happy for her as well.

This semester it was really difficult accepting my break-up with Nini. (Note: I saw it as a break. Nini was the one who found a new boyfriend and made it a break-*up*.) Dealing with my parents' break-up as well made everything worse. If it was up to me, my parents would be living in the same house, in Salt Lake City, and we'd sit down together to eat every night. Then I would hang out with Nini writing songs on my guitar, or hang out with Big Red crushing marauders and zombies. It's just hard getting used to change, I guess.

Before my mom left, she threw me a curveball.

"We're really looking forward to seeing you over the holidays," she said, hugging me goodbye. "If you want to come. It's up to you, of course."

Uh-oh. Does this mean I have to choose? I wondered.

My dad is trying to get better at cooking, but our Monday-night dinner is not exactly *MasterChef*—unless the master in question is Chef Boyardee. Dad is squinting at the permission slip from Miss Jenn about the convention this weekend. He's in denial about needing reading glasses.

"This is kind of short notice," he says, mixing up his pasta with a fork. It's still nuclear hot from the microwave. "But I'm fine with you going, if you really want to."

"Everyone's going. It's a *High School Musical* convention."

"Better take headphones," Dad jokes. "I suspect it will be *loud*."

I manage to eat a few mouthfuls of what might be beef ravioli without burning my mouth. Nini's moms will have made something delicious for dinner tonight. My mom will have made something delicious, except she's cooking in Chicago. For her and Todd.

"So," my dad says, grinding some black pepper onto

his plate. "Your mom and I were wondering about your winter break."

I have a bad feeling about where this is going, so I cram more ravioli into my mouth until I feel like a chipmunk in a field of tomatoes.

"We want it to be your choice," he says. "Whatever you want, we support. Whatever you want to do, I mean. Wherever you want to go."

"You mean, to college?" I ask, mouth still full. I know that isn't what he means. Dad shifts in his chair as though he can't get comfortable. There's so much pepper on his food now, it's probably inedible.

"We know that this is hard for you," he says. "Your first holiday season with parents who are separated. Parents who aren't together anymore."

"I know what *separated* means," I tell him.

"Sure. Good. Of course you do."

This is one of the worst things about parents splitting up. They keep wanting to Have Conversations About Serious Things. I miss the days when Dad and I drove around blasting old songs by Cheap Trick and KISS, or when Mom spent an entire Saturday making a papier-mâché volcano for my Warhammer armies. (The volcano ended up under my bed, growing mold.) I miss conversations about what happened at school or work that day. I miss conversations about Star Wars or the annoying barking dog next door.

"So what I'm saying," Dad tells me, "or what *we're* saying is, it's your call."

"What is?"

"Staying here for the holidays or going to Chicago."

I guess it hasn't really sunk in until now. Mom isn't coming back to Salt Lake, not even for Christmas. If I want to see her, I have to fly east. And if I want to see her, I have to see Todd as well.

"What will you do?" I ask him.

"Don't worry about me."

"You can't spend the holidays alone," I say.

"I could go to your aunt's house, the way we do at Thanksgiving."

"And what about the rest of the time?"

"I have plenty of things to do," Dad says. "Jobs around the house. Movies. Bowling. I'll be pretty busy. If you decide to go, that is. And if you decide to stay here for the holidays, that's fine as well. No pressure."

Here's the thing. I know that my parents are trying to make it easier for me. But just saying "no pressure" doesn't mean anything. Do I spend Christmas with Mom or Dad? Do I spend half the winter break here in SLC and half in Chicago? All my friends are here. Nini is here.

I don't want to hurt my mom by saying I'd rather stay home, with my friends and with Dad. She might see it as some kind of punishment, like I want to make her suffer for the break-up. I wish nobody had to suffer, especially when my parents are acting all mature and calm, and not screaming at each other the way I've heard other separated parents do. One kid at school said he had to go to court because his parents were fighting about how he spent the holidays. He ended up spending most of Christmas Day being driven from Utah to New Mexico by some uncle so he could see his dad.

"Ricky?" My dad must have asked me something I didn't hear.

"Sorry. Just thinking," I say. Just thinking random thoughts that lead nowhere, I want to tell him. How can I let my parents know that I love them both and don't want to hurt anyone's feelings? We're not the kind of family that talks about things like love. Nini and her moms are always saying *I love you*, but we're more reserved in this family. Uptight, I guess.

"Take your time," Dad says. "You don't have to decide right now. Maybe after you get back from the school trip? So your mom and I can plan."

"Sure," I say, glad this conversation is over. For now. It

would be way easier if my parents make this decision for me, but I don't think they're going to oblige.

And now there's a shadow over the trip to the convention. When I get back, I'll have to make the big announcement that will disappoint one of them. Great.

Maybe the convention will be so amazing that I won't have time to think. Overthinking never helps. I'll have such a good time with Nini and Big Red and everyone else that I'll forget I have a decision to make at all.

I'll forget this is the first time in my entire life when I won't be with both my parents over the winter break. If this is growing up, it sucks.

Insta Interlude

Following

E.J. checking in with an update re our journey. Actual and spiritual. Remember I mentioned a road trip to Wyoming? That's right, Insta-buddies, we're going to *High School Musical: The Musical: The Convention* this weekend.

Now for the good news: I'm driving myself. I can drive my own car to Wyoming. I'm eighteen now. Full unrestricted license. No more school van for me. This is now a genuine road trip.

And there ain't no road trip like an E.J. Caswell road trip, 'cause an E.J. Caswell road trip don't stop.

E.J. out.

402 likes

Add a comment...

CHAPTER SIX

NINI

For a semester-long History project we've been working in pairs on research. The topic is Collaborations that Changed the World, and we're all up to our third and final assignment. Kourtney and I have been working as a pair—of course—and without boasting, I can honestly say we've been rocking it. We've got some healthy (read: fight-to-the-death) competition going on with Ricky and Big Red, and we're determined to get our third straight A for this.

Our first "collaboration" subjects were Elizabeth Cady Stanton and Susan B. Anthony; we explored how they led the women's suffrage movement of the nineteenth century.

"You know, they don't have to be all-female collaborations," Big Red tells us, leaning across from his desk. "It's not just women who changed the world."

Kourtney gives him her trademark glare. She doesn't have to say a word, because that look alone has Big Red trembling in his high-tops.

"I mean, um . . ." he stammers, "I know that women have done amazing things. And you know, if there was a historic woman skateboarder, say, then . . ."

"You and Ricky would do a report on her?" Kourtney pounces. She and I have prepped for this.

"Of course," says Big Red, all earnest, and Ricky nods along. He's got more sense than to take Kourtney on.

"Then I assume," says Kourtney, eyes boring holes in Big Red's face, "that you're already researching Patti McGee, the first professional female skateboarder, born in 1945, and her collaboration with the Hobie company."

Big Red has no answer. Ricky just sighs. But our teacher, Ms. Jones, happens to be passing by and hears the conversation.

"No living subjects, please!" she admonishes. "This is a history class! Boys, you need to think beyond the skateboard. And, girls—what's your plan for this assignment?"

"We're thinking the abolitionist Harriet Tubman,"

I tell her. "And maybe her collaboration with Colonel James Montgomery during the Civil War. She was the first woman to lead an armed assault during the war."

"Now that's more like it," Ms. Jones says, frowning at Ricky and Big Red, and moves on to break up an argument on the next aisle. Two pairs of kids are trying to claim sole rights to Antony and Cleopatra.

That all happened a few weeks ago. I haven't given too much thought to our final project, maybe because now I'm obsessed with my secret project at the *HSM* convention. I really want it to be a big romantic gesture, one that will blow Ricky away. Then, when I tell him the news about Denver, he'll know how much I care about him, and won't think I'm abandoning him.

School goes on, and History waits for no one. In class we have a visitor, Ms. Jones tells us, because she's concerned our research interests are too narrow: None of us, over the course of the previous two assignments, have picked any historic collaborations from the *sciences*.

As soon as she says the S-word, we know what's in store: Mr. Mazzara, in his gray cardigan and pants with the pleats ironed in, standing in front of the board.

"Students," he says. "Ms. Jones tells me that you may need some encouragement and ideas about famous scientific collaborations."

One group reveals their plans to study Benjamin Franklin and the mouse he sent up in a kite to discover electricity. Mr. Mazzara looks unimpressed.

"I believe you're talking about an animated movie," he says. "Mice are not collaborators."

Now Ricky raises his hand.

"Why can't mice be our collaborators, Mr. Mazzara? Aren't we all animals?" Everyone starts giggling and shuffling around.

"I am not here to debate the nature and qualities of the mouse," Mr. Mazzara says in his most pompous voice, though he looks ready to launch into a diatribe/biology lesson.

"Ricky," says Ms. Jones, interrupting just in time. "No time-wasting, please."

Usually I would shoot Ricky a grin, but right now I'm feeling a little awkward around him. Maybe it's because I'm keeping a massive secret from him, and I'm afraid I might give it away.

Ms. Jones continues, "Mr. Mazzara, would you give us some examples of important scientific collaborations?"

"Of course." Mr. Mazzara smiles, and we all recoil. I don't think I've ever seen him smile. It looks unnatural. "All we have to do is scan the lists of the Nobel Prize winners to see some stellar examples. An excellent topic would be James P. Allison and Tasuku Honjo, who won a Nobel prize in 2018 for their work fighting cancer."

"Are there any women scientists you would recommend?" Kourtney asks, with a sideways grimace at Big Red.

"Of course, of course." Mr. Mazzara is rocking on his heels with enthusiasm. "Marie Curie remains the only person to have been awarded the Nobel Prize for two different sciences, chemistry and physics. As you all know, Madame Curie not only coined the term *radioactivity*, she discovered two new elements, radium and polonium. Her collaborator, for the purposes of your assignment, was her husband, Pierre Curie."

"That might be cool," Kourtney whispers to me.

"Another example," Mr. Mazzara explains, "from an earlier era is Ada Lovelace. She was a British mathematician in the early nineteenth century, and is considered to be the world's first computer programmer. Her collaborator was another mathematician, Charles Babbage."

"But how could they program computers when computers weren't invented yet?" asks Big Red.

"Maybe they dreamed big," Kourtney says. "Maybe they imagined something nobody knew."

"Exactly so." Mr. Mazzara bows his head. "They created an algorithm that could only be carried out by a machine. Ada Lovelace realized that machines could do more than crunch numbers, as it were. As well as to calculate, machines had the capacity to compute.

"This is what scientists do," Mr. Mazzara says. "They imagine what isn't there. They step into the unknown. They may create or develop something that leads to other scientific discoveries and advances. The fruits of their labor may be reaped only years later. Decades later. Centuries later, perhaps."

"But we need to reap the fruits of our labor this semester," Ricky points out. "We only have a couple of weeks."

"Then you all better start working at once," Ms. Jones says in her no-nonsense voice. "Thanks so much for dropping by, Mr. Mazzara."

"Remember, students, if you have any questions, the door to the Robotics Lab is always open," he says. "Apart from evenings and weekends, and whenever I'm not there to supervise. We have a lot of expensive equipment. And *someone* . . ."

He looks hard at Ricky and pauses for effect.

"*Someone* managed to jam one of the new computers just after they were installed earlier this semester."

After he leaves, we all huddle in our teams again, talking about the assignment. I'm really interested in this

Ada Lovelace, and luckily so is Kourtney. Her eyes are shining.

"Pretty cool, right?" she says. "Who knew that Mr. Mazzara could be so inspirational?"

"Maybe he has more in common with Miss Jenn than they realize," I joke. "They both like talking about imagining things and building for the future. And I really liked what you said, Kourt."

"What did I say?"

"About them dreaming big. I guess everyone we've studied so far has been a dreamer."

"They got things done as well," she points out. "They made things happen. It's not enough just to sit around dreaming. At some point you have to *do* something."

"Like this assignment," I say, and Ms. Jones says we can all go to the library to start our research.

It's on the walk there that it hits me. If I go to school in Denver next semester, it's not just Ricky I'll be leaving behind. It's Kourtney, too. Who will she pair with next semester on projects like this one? Who will she sit with, and confide in? I've been so nervous about going to a new place where I don't know anybody, and so excited about the opportunities I'll have there, that I've forgotten what this means for Kourtney. She's been my BFF forever. That won't change. But she's been so supportive of me this whole time, listening to all my anxieties and fears and dreams.

What about *her* dreams?

And what kind of friend am I if I don't support and encourage her, like Mr. Mazzara said, to step into the unknown?

CHAPTER SEVEN

CARLOS

All week I'm carrying the burden. And no, I don't mean my new tortoiseshell glasses, which are huge and incredibly flattering, but so heavy I feel a dent forming on the bridge of my nose.

No, I mean the burden of being East High's resident *High School Musical* historian, and confidant-slash-choreographer to Miss Jenn. Don't get me wrong: #IHeartMissJenn. But this week she has the energy of a hummingbird that's had one too many Pepsis, and whenever she sees Mr. Mazzara walking her way, she leaps into the nearest room—even if that room is the janitor's closet—and drags me with her.

"Carlos," she tells me. "You are the only one who truly

understands the significance of this convention. Everyone else thinks of it as a road trip. A fun time. A class trip."

"Infidels," I mutter, shaking my head.

"I know, right?" She grips my sleeve. I swear that the white leatherette of my mustard letter jacket has sweaty fingerprints embedded in it that I will *never* be able to clean. "This weekend is our Xanadu."

At first I'm not entirely sure what she means. *Xanadu* is a movie my grandma likes, because it has Olivia Newton-John and roller skates, two of her favorite things. This is why I love hanging out with my grandma. She has opinions on every movie musical ever made. Although she loves O N-J, she doesn't love *Grease*. She says a *buena chica* like Sandy shouldn't waste her time with a boy who wears a leather jacket to school. My own personal issue with *Grease* is that all the leads are supposed to be at high school, but they're clearly, like, thirty years old. Grandma says that was how it was in the old days, and next I'll be complaining that the actress who played Liesl in *The Sound of Music* wasn't really sixteen going on seventeen.

(FYI: The actress was Charmian Carr, and she was twenty-two going on twenty-three when they filmed that movie. I learned that from Google, not Grandma.)

"What do you mean?" I ask Miss Jenn. She's still doing her dramatic-pause thing, her eyes really big. She's leaning against the janitor's mop, so it looks as though she has a ratty white weave.

"Xanadu, Carlos. The most beautiful place on earth. The realization of all our dreams."

I guess I must look dubious. The realization of all my dreams is Broadway, not a ski resort in an underpopulated Western state.

"Haven't you seen *Citizen Kane*?" she asks.

"Is it a musical?"

Miss Jenn sighs.

"'In Xanadu did Kubla Khan / A stately pleasure-dome decree,'" she recites. I've heard of *Chaka* Khan, I want to tell her, but she grips my arm again. Outside the closet we can hear Mr. Mazzara's voice, asking if anyone has seen Miss Jenn. We lock eyes and don't make a peep. Then another teacher calls Mr. Mazzara's name and the moment of danger passes.

"Okay," Miss Jenn whispers, leaning close. "We have two missions when we're at the convention this weekend. We need a guest star for our spring musical."

I try not to gasp too loud. "You mean a real-life *HSM* cast member? Aside from you, that is?"

Miss Jenn bats the second-too-late compliment away.

"I was chorus line. I'm hoping for a name character. So I'll work my contacts, old friends from set, and so forth. But you need to impress as well. You're a future Fosse."

"Blankenbuehler."

"What now?"

"Andy Blankenbuehler. My grandmother took me to see *In the Heights* in Chicago when I was nine. That's when I knew I wanted to do more than dance—I wanted to be a choreographer."

"Blankenbuehler," Miss Jenn says. "I wonder if he's related to Ferris Bueller?"

I have no idea what she's talking about.

"Just kidding." She rolls her eyes. "Wasn't he the choreographer for *Hamilton* as well? Nice taste, Carlos. You continue to astound me. Now you need to astound the *HSM* stars. And we need everyone in their East High jackets at all times. We need to turn those emotional screws . . . or whatever. I'm not very mechanical."

"We could appoint Kourtney to the job of school-spirit police," I suggest. "She could make sure everyone stays on-message, clothes-wise."

"Good point. We need all hands on deck. We have

to wow. We can't just be fans there for a sing-along. Everything we do has to impress. We need to be professional, we need to be polished, we need to be fresh. I can pull strings, but I need good puppets. I want to get that special guest. We *have* to get one."

"Have to?" I'm as starstruck as the next *HSM*er, but Miss Jenn seems to be on a whole other plane of fandesperation. "I mean, we can still have a show without a special guest, right?"

Miss Jenn look horrified.

"We can have a *show*," she says. "If you mean a school production."

"Yeah" is all I can say to this. Let's be real, people. West of the Rockies is not exactly off-off-Broadway.

She grips my arm. "Carlos, we can have so much more. Don't you see? I thought you of all people would understand what we could do here with a little star power. I want to take this Drama department to the next level. The school name is already famous. We could become a performing-arts magnet. Think about it."

I'm thinking.

"Imagine our school," Miss Jenn continues in a stage whisper, "as a place all the best young singers and dancers and writers and directors in the West wanted to go.

Imagine how casting directors would want to visit, to pick *our* talent for shows and movies."

"That would be amazing," I say/sigh. Because it would. I wouldn't be the only student in this school who lived and breathed musical theater. There would be a whole Carlos chorus line.

"It'd be like Juilliard," says Miss Jenn, her eyes wide. "Except younger and at a higher altitude."

"You really think it's possible?" I ask her, and she nods, long and slow.

"We've made a phenomenal start. If we knock this next show out of the park, or whatever it is they say . . ."

No idea.

". . . then we can make a great case to the school board for upscaling the program and advertising regionally for the most talented students this side of the Continental Divide. They won't be able to say no. They'd be *crazy* to say no."

"So," I say, understanding her point at last, "we need the star power to light a spark."

"We do indeed. This is our big chance. We can't blow it. Will you help me this weekend?"

We shake on it. I love the idea of really putting our school on the map, not just as the place *HSM* was filmed, but where the most talented showkids study. All of a sudden, my future starts looking Technicolor. Miss Jenn eases the door open. The coast looks clear. I wriggle out, trying to avoid the metal pail and mile-wide broom. Miss Jenn follows, her high heels clacking on the polished floor.

And there's Mr. Mazzara, like a puppet himself, popping up out of nowhere. He does that quizzical-eyebrow thing he does.

"New office, Miss Jenn?" he asks. "Or are you looking for props?"

"I'd love to stay and chitchat," she replies, brazening it out. "But I have work to do. Urgent work."

She hurries away down the hallway, going in the opposite direction from her office. I swerve out of Mr. M's way.

"Like getting special training to drive the school van?" he calls after her, but Miss Jenn keeps scurrying away. "A four-hour course! You need to take a four-hour course!"

I head off in search of Seb, to whisper to him about my not-so-secret mission. The bad and sad news: Seb really can't go on the trip. He told me again this morning that this weekend is the be-all and end-all for cows-all, and he really needs to help his family out. I tried not to be too upset, and it's great that he has such a strong bond with his parents. His entire family turned up to see the show.

#HSMCon won't be the same without him. It'll be all business for me, helping Miss Jenn to secure her guest star for whatever musical she decides we're doing. All work, no play. Sigh.

CHAPTER EIGHT

BIG RED

Usually Wednesday nights are quiet at Salt Lake Slices. That's the pizzeria my family owns. My grandfather started the business and now my parents run it. But tonight it's just me, my mother, and a guy called Sandy who works the oven.

Sandy's kind of a jerk, in my opinion. According to him, he's been a competitive BMX rider, a competitive skateboarder, and a competitive surfer. "Semipro, dude," he tells me. "Back in Cal." I've never found any evidence online. I've also never heard him say the entire word *California*.

My mom secretly agrees with me about Sandy, I think, but she says that Sandy is good at slinging dough and hauling pizzas in and out of the big wood-burning oven. We're pretty short-staffed right now, especially on weekends.

This is midweek, and Tuesdays and Wednesdays aren't busy nights. There's usually me or someone else working the counter and busing tables, and Sandy making pizzas. My mother's here tonight doing the wages out back. I'm just trying to concentrate on taking the right orders and giving the right change. Maybe tap-dancing a little, when I think no one is looking.

Unfortunately, Sandy is looking.

"Nice heel drop, bro," he comments, sliding a pizza into its box. "Not sure about your shuffle."

Trust Sandy to know the terminology. He's probably a "semipro" tap dancer as well. He hands me the box and I pass it to the waiting delivery driver. Sandy could hand it over himself, but he's too lazy to step up to the counter.

"My style's funkier than yours, I'd say," he tells me, though I haven't said anything to him, and I'm pretending to be busy, refilling the napkin holder. "Someone told me once I could be the next Savion Glover."

Your mother? I want to say, but luckily a couple of customers walk in, and we get busy.

Tonight I just need to get through my shift. One good thing about work: It takes my mind off Ashlyn. Things have been . . . not strained exactly, but weird. Since the show. Since we kissed. I still can't believe we did that. I'm not like Ricky, ready to put everything out there. When he stood up at the musical audition and sang a song to Nini, right in front of everyone, with Nini looking incredulous and E.J. in a rage, I was in awe of him. Ricky may be rash sometimes, but I have to hand it to him—he's brave. Me? Not so much. Maybe it's because I've never had a girlfriend.

I really like Ashlyn; she's funny and talented, and she's not a show-off or a fake. If she kissed me, she must like me, too. Right? I don't know. Girls are mysteries.

We hustle through some orders, and I realize I'm humming a tune. I wasn't even in the musical, but somehow I know all the words. I'm ringing up an order and "Start of Something New" dances through my brain. And then, just like that, I might be saying "Extra pepperoni, right?" but I'm thinking about Ashlyn again.

This weekend is the trip to the convention. At school I just see Ashlyn in passing, and everyone is rushing around because it's the end of the semester, and they have their charity concert coming up. But we'll all be packed into a van going up to the convention, and then we'll be staying the whole weekend in the hotel. We're going to see each other all the time. What if she's sorry about the kiss? What if she's changed her mind?

I should have asked Ricky about this. He has way more experience than I do. He and Nini went out for almost a year before the "summer disaster," as he calls it. But I would feel stupid. We don't usually talk about things like that. And what would I say? *Hey, Ricky, does a kiss mean that Ashlyn and I are a couple, or what?*

Anyway, I know what he'd tell me: *Why don't you just talk to Ashlyn?*

Easy for him to say. I'm not the smooth-talking type. I'm not even the smooth-texting type. In a lull between orders, I decide to send Ashlyn a "casual" text.

Attempt one: Hey!

I delete this. The exclamation point is trying way too hard.

Attempt two: Hey—how's it going?

This I delete as well. It reads like spam, like someone's phishing for your bank details.

Attempt three: Hey, I'm at work tonight. What are you doing?

Delete. Sounds creepy, as though I'm stalking her, or trying to control her life.

Attempt four: Hey—how are things? I'm at work.

Maybe? No. Delete. This text makes me seem like the most boring person west of the Rockies. Why can't I write something casual and funny and non-boring and not trying too hard? Maybe that's the problem. I'm trying too hard. I'm thinking too hard.

Song titles. That might be cute. Or is that too cute?

Attempt five: Pizza is "what I've been looking for" tonight.

Delete, delete, mega-delete. I sound deranged. I sound foolish. I sound as though someone crazy, who hates me, has stolen my phone and is trying to humiliate me.

There's only one thing for it.

Attempt six: Hey.

That's good. Calm. Casual. Not too needy. Not too weird. Not too are-we-a-couple-because-we-kissed-once-please-explain.

Send. And now the wait begins. What if she doesn't reply? What if she replies with something like *Lose this number* or *Busy right now with real friends* or . . .

My mom emerges from the storeroom.

"Bad news, I'm afraid," she tells me. "Most of the staff seem to be traveling for the holidays already, and we have a big hole on Saturday night. We might need you here."

"But I have the convention," I remind her.

"I know. Maybe someone will change their plans. But you were on the schedule, remember? And now everyone else is saying they can't fill in for you."

I am so bummed. The decision to go to the *HSM*

convention *was* last-minute. It's true that I was already down to work this Saturday.

"I'm so sorry, bud," my mom says. "I know I signed the permission form for you, but it looks like it has to be you and me here this weekend."

There's nothing I can do. This is a family business. It's small, and our family works long hours to keep it going. It's my responsibility as well. How can I justify going off to have fun at the convention, leaving everyone here in the lurch? Saturday is our busy night.

My phone buzzes. A reply from Ashlyn.

Hey—looking forward to this weekend.

This weekend. How can I tell her I'm not going to be there? She may think I'm bailing out because I don't want to spend time together. Because I regret the kiss. What kind of text can communicate *Glad we kissed but I have to blow off this weekend*?

Just when I think tonight couldn't be any weirder, I clear the table by the window and happen to glance out at the parking lot. Outside there's a van with East High in big blue letters. It kinda looks like someone's learning to drive, because the van is reversing into a space, then pulling out again to do a three-point turn and reverse into another space. We have a big parking lot, and this isn't the first time I've seen someone have a driving lesson out there. Sometimes it's a kid I know from school with his mother or father. Sometimes they get pizza before they drive away.

But this is the first time it doesn't look like a kid from school. It looks like . . . No, it can't be. Is that Miss Jenn and Mr. Mazzara trying to park the van?

CHAPTER NINE

Miss Jenn's Top Seven Rules for
Getting through Four Hours of
Specialist Van-Driving Training,
as Mandated by the Board of
Education and Principal Gutierrez

1. Do not complain. Suck it up and buckle in. Remember that four hours is shorter than watching *Les Misérables* on Broadway (including the interval and post-show lingering at the gift-shop counter). Sing "Start of Something New" to lift your spirits.

2. Get to the second line of the chorus and realize that the song is totally inappropriate, because Mr. Mazzara is your driving instructor. If you try to make it Mazzara-appropriate, he won't appreciate it. And nothing rhymes with *robotics* anyway.

3. Try not to lose your cool when Mr. Mazzara reminds you to use your side mirrors. Remind him that you've been driving since Britney Spears released "Oops! . . . I Did It Again" and Madonna got married in a Scottish castle. Don't smirk when Mr. Mazzara pretends he hasn't heard of either. You just know that boy grew up glued to the Mouseketeers, singing along and swinging his knitted tie. Don't snap when he says you're older than he thought. Don't react when he tells you that driving a van is a more serious business than driving (his words) "a car that looks like a peppermint."

4. Keep paying attention. Don't let negative thoughts intrude, the ones about this being the intermission of your life, and you have to have a great second act. You *have* to. That's why taking this conference by storm and luring a star to your spring musical is so important. Everyone's on a high after the musical. But it's just a high-school high. You want a performing-arts-hub high. You want an *influencer* high. You want a high that somehow leads to a red carpet, or a yellow-brick road.

5. All Mr. Mazzara wants is another three-point turn. Smile. He has no idea about the many glittering points of a star, like the one you're going to see this weekend and talk into an East High cameo.

6. Remind yourself that four hours of van hell on the streets of Salt Lake City on Wednesday = five hours of van joy driving to Wyoming on Friday. With ten theater kids. To follow your star. To take over the world.

7. Don't be startled when you are reverse-parking for the hundredth time in the lot of Salt Lake Slices and think you see one of your students staring at you, openmouthed, through the window. Smile and toss your hair. This could end up on Instagram. Note to self: That line could be your motto: *This could end up on Instagram.* All the world's a stage, after all. Even the parking lot of a pizza joint. Even the driver's seat of a high-school van.

CHAPTER TEN

SEB

It was a big deal for me stepping into the limelight as Sharpay, but this semester has been all about stepping up. I've made new friends. I also made myself step away from the piano—not to mention the milking shed—and finally act on my obsession with musical theater.

Kourtney and I have a lunch date to talk about the *HSM* convention. We need to plan what she'll be doing there.

"And what *you're* doing," she says, setting her tray on the table and making me scooch along. "I mean, you could do a vocal class, you could do one of the piano master classes. People need to hear you, Sebbie. Not just the cows in your barn."

"The thing is," I tell her, "I can't go this weekend."

"What?" she practically shouts, her earrings jingling as though an earthquake has hit the school.

"It's okay," I say. It's not really, but what can I do?

In my family I'm not quite the same as everyone else, in so many ways. I love musical theater more than I love cattle and sheep. My parents were really supportive when I was in the show. I mean, they bought out three entire rows of the bleachers. They made the craziest signs. There was rainbow-colored glitter everywhere in the carpet of our house for the next week.

But sometimes cattle and sheep really are more important than anything else. We have the final stock sale of the year coming up on Saturday morning, and it's a big one. I have to be there to help.

"They support me," I tell Kourtney, "and I support them. That's the way families work, right?"

"I guess." Kourtney mock-pouts at me, toying with the vivid yellow macaroni cheese on her tray. "I can't believe it's the same weekend. Shouldn't cows be hibernating or something for the winter?"

"Cattle and sheep are every day, not just for Christmas," I say, and we both laugh, in spite of ourselves.

"Carlos must be really sad," she says.

"He's frantic right now. He and Miss Jenn are on some kind of overdrive. He told me they have a secret mission."

"Can you dish?" Kourtney leans in.

"Officially, no. And unofficially, I don't really understand what's going on anyway. Carlos is picking up all Miss Jenn's crazy energy."

"Big Red says he saw Miss Jenn test-driving the school van last night. And you know who her driving instructor was? Mr. Mazzara!"

"No wonder she's in a whirl," I say. The whole cafeteria feels as though it's buzzing with excitement, even though only eleven people are going to the convention with Miss Jenn. Ten in the van, plus E.J. driving himself. *Room for me,* I keep thinking. *If only . . .*

"We don't have to talk about this weekend," Kourtney says. She stabs at her juice box with a straw. "I don't want you to have to listen to me make plans, when you're going to miss it."

"Kourtney." I look her square in the eyes. "I'm not that kind of friend. And one thing I know from cattle sales is you need to be organized, you need to be up early, and you need to keep everything moving."

"Are you talking about actual cows here?" Kourtney looks icked-out.

"Steers, mainly, but you get the idea."

"Okay," she says, sounding doubtful. "I'm going to ask you for advice, and please be totally honest. Nini has been my best friend for, like, *forever*, and when I ask her she just tells me I'm the greatest and can do everything."

"Nini is right," I tell her.

"Please! Remember when you told me you didn't think I should quit makeup crew?"

I shake my head. That is not what I said. Not at all. I'll never forgot gazing up at Kourtney (she was sitting on the stairs), still in awe of her at that point. I mean, totally in awe.

"What I said was, you have a gift for making things look better," I remind her. "The makeup you created for me to play Sharpay was amazing. And that sequined coat with the blue boa? You could be a professional. However—"

"That's the thing," she interrupts. "Nini wants me to sign up for vocal workshops at the convention, but don't you think makeup and wardrobe are where my talent really lies?"

You know, so many people give the wrong impression of themselves. I guess I'm one of them. To most of the non-theater kids at school, I'm a clean-cut farm kid who wears button-down shirts and rushes home every day for chores.

Kourtney is another one. She seems so together, so no-nonsense. But inside she has her moments of doubt. Who knew?

I take her hand.

"The reason I asked you that question back then, about if you were planning to quit makeup crew, was because I heard you sing at the tech rehearsal in that spooky old theater. Everyone there was blown away, remember? Miss Jenn got that somewhere-over-the-rainbow look in her eyes. That's when I realized you're multitalented."

Kourtney gazes down at the table in an adorable *aw-shucks* way.

"You're like me," I tell her, and she glances up, smiling at me.

"I wish I was like you, Sebbie. You really are multitalented. You're the most amazing singer and dancer."

"That's not what I meant," I tell her. "I mean, people used to think of us in one way. In my case, I was always behind the piano. You were behind—"

"The makeup brush," Kourtney says, and we both laugh.

"Right. So we have to step into the spotlight. It's hard. I didn't think I could do it, but somehow I did. And now you have to, in the spring musical. So . . ."

"Really?" Kourtney still looks dubious.

"This Saturday. Vocal workshops," I command, though I'm not very good at being commanding. Carlos is better at this. It's his dance-captain military experience.

"They'll probably be full," Kourtney says. "But I'll try. The beginners' workshop, anyway."

"Promise?"

She nods. "I just wish you were going to be there."

I wish I could be there as well. All that time to spend with Carlos—it would be a dream. And I love seeing Carlos in his element. It's my element as well now. But wishing is something for birthday cakes. This Saturday I'll be with steers rather than with stars, but that's okay. Family first.

I remember what Carlos said to me, right before I went onstage as Sharpay. *Count your blessings*, he said. That's what I have to do right now, be thankful that I have Carlos in my life, and Kourtney, and all the theater kids. There'll be other *HSM* conventions—maybe—and there'll be another musical in the spring.

The night of the show, Carlos also told me to dance my heart out. On Saturday afternoon, I'll be dancing alone in the barn, pretending it's a stage, or the convention hotel. Perhaps a little of the *HSM* magic will drift through the air, and turn the hay beneath my feet into a magic carpet.

Insta Interlude

E.J. here, in case you didn't know.

So today my drama teacher said that no one was allowed to ride shotgun with me. To Wyoming. Everyone's parental permission slips are for the school van only. E.J. will be driving there solo.

Solo—but not sad face. No! Remember when I said it was time in my life for soul-searching? Well, this is the perfect opportunity. I get some me-time, which is rare. I take the role of Senior Class Treasurer seriously, so it's a lot of responsibility. The more I think about it, the more I realize that I'm always with other people and about other people. Captaining a team. Starring in a cast. Leading a group. It's always other people, all the time.

This trip can really and truly be about me. Four hours plus each way, all by myself. Time to play the music I want. Think my thoughts. And you know I can rest my voice and be ready to hit the convention in top form.

I got to go check on my winter tires and fill the tank with gas. I've already plotted out where I'll stop en route. (Shout out, Pocatello, Idaho!) Once a Boy Scout, always a Boy Scout.

E.J. out.

550 likes

Add a comment...

CHAPTER ELEVEN

NINI

We'll have fun this weekend at the convention with the whole gang, but it's a shame that E.J. is driving himself up to Wyoming. He's been so cool about me and Ricky getting back together, and giving up the lead to Ricky was beyond unselfish. He's really a great guy. And now I think about it, E.J. driving is a smart move on his part. Better than being crammed into a van for five hours with a lot of overexcited people.

Most overexcited person: me. I have so much planned for #HSMCon, maybe too much. Kourtney and I have been plotting for days about the best way for me to get all the signatures. I hope Ricky will be surprised and happy about it.

Another reason I'm overexcited: nerves. I don't want to spoil this weekend in any way by mentioning the YAC opportunity to Ricky. We've all worked hard and need to have some fun, not worry about the future.

Friday afternoon the bell rings at 3:10. We assemble in the school parking lot with too much luggage, too many heavy coats, and way too much excitement. Kourtney and I give big hugs to Seb and Big Red, who can't come with us. That is so unfair. It won't be the same without them.

E.J. drives away, waving at us.

"I was going to ask him if he wanted to drive in a convoy with us," Miss Jenn says, sounding disappointed. I knew he was planning on leaving first, because I saw him run to his car. He's super excited about getting to the convention as well. "Bye, E.J.! See you there!"

"I just hope we get there in time to sign up for the sessions tomorrow," says Kourtney. She leans in, her voice low. "And we can start getting some of the signatures you need. Corbin Bleu is only there tonight."

"I *have* to get him!" I whisper back. "Ricky would be so thrilled!"

"Let's go, people," calls Miss Jenn, and we cram into the back of the van with our bags, singing our own version of "What Time Is It?" It goes like this:

What time is it?
Wintertime!
Our HSM convention!
What time is it?
Cosplay time!
We'll show off our invention!

Mr. Mazzara is there to supervise us packing the van, making sure we all buckle our seat belts. I don't think he trusts Miss Jenn.

"This is a standard fifteen-seat van," he drones, tapping his clipboard. (What? Why does he have a clipboard?) "If you would please all stop singing for a moment, I will demonstrate the safety features of this vehicle."

"This is a van, not a plane," Natalie murmurs to Miss Jenn, and I can't help laughing.

"And driving is far more dangerous than flying," he insists, and we all groan. Except for Miss Jenn.

"Luckily for us," she chirps, "musicals save lives. Now please, we need to get on the road."

"Snow is in the forecast!" Mr. Mazzara booms through the door, right before Miss Jenn closes it. She gives Mr. Mazzara a thumbs-up, which he doesn't return.

"He's right about the snow," Natalie says, checking her phone. "But it should be light. We'll be okay."

"Snow is in the air indeed," says Miss Jenn. "And stardust! Two reasons I'm wearing my fake-fur gilet. So long, farewell, auf Wiedersehen, adieu!"

Mr. Mazzara stands watching us as we drive away. He looks worried.

What Mr. Mazzara doesn't know: We decided to . . . ah . . . *customize* the school van. Carlos had the idea, and he and Seb and Kourtney have been working on it. As soon as we're out of sight of school, we get Miss Jenn to pull over. Then we scramble out of the van and apply transfer stickers to each side. Luckily our van is already red and white, so we just need to tape on some signs and a Wildcats pennant flag.

"All this needs," Kourtney says, "is a little more *HSM* flair."

"We're going to look like the real thing," Natalie tells Carlos, taking a picture for Insta.

"We *are* the real thing!" he says. "And Kourtney has our costumes so we can all look the part this weekend. We need to be red letters all the way."

"Seb did an amazing job with this Wildcats logo," I say, squeezing Carlos's hand. He's been quiet in an un-Carlos-like way this week, ever since he knew for sure that Seb couldn't come to the convention with us.

"Wildcats back in the van!" Miss Jenn calls, and we're all glad to get in: The weather is turning. The sky is a thick gray blanket and there's not much daylight left. Streetlights cast pools of yellow in the gloom.

"Brrrr," says Ricky, climbing into the van after me. "Mr. M was right about that forecast."

"We'll have to warm up with a sing-along," Ashlyn suggests.

"After we get on I-15," says Miss Jenn. "I need to listen to the GPS lady."

"I know the way," Natalie tells her. She's riding shotgun and has her own clipboard with a printout of our route. It's good we have our very own stage manager on board. "I-15 to Idaho Falls, then east through Teton Pass, past the Swan Valley. We could take the Snake River route, but it's longer."

"Sounds so theatrical," says Miss Jenn. "Swan Valley! Snake River!"

"I think you missed the turnoff for the highway," Natalie says.

"Good start," Gina says with a grin. She's sitting with Ashlyn. It's so cool that E.J. bought Gina a ticket to come back to SLC, and that Ashlyn invited Gina to stay with her after opening night. This is what friendship means: helping each other out. Whatever ups and downs we've had this semester, Gina is one of us now. I'm so glad she's on this road trip with us.

Ricky's sitting in the row by himself, the seat next to him taken up with his guitar case. Kourtney and I need to conspire for a while about this weekend, but at some point I want to swap places with the guitar. I know how much Ricky's looking forward to this trip, and he's disappointed that Big Red can't come to the convention.

Which is why I haven't mentioned that I might be going to school in Denver next semester. I've sworn Kourtney to silence. Ricky is still getting used to his parents being separated. I know I have to tell him, but nothing wrong with waiting until after this trip. Have a fun weekend. Besides, I'm on a mission. I need to get signatures for Ricky's surprise gift. And more alerts keep popping up on all our phones to give us more details about the schedule.

> Bop to the Top with Ashley T: Sharpay in the house for two hours only Sat @HSMCon!

Chem Club latest: Monique Coleman
@HSMCon Sat AM only

Don't miss your audition slot with Ms.
Darbus! Alyson Reed @HSMCon Sat
afternoon!

I have to make a plan of action. Forget workshops and panels: I'm going to be Meet-and-Greet Queen. It'll mean not doing everything with Ricky, so he doesn't guess what I'm up to, but there's plenty of other things to keep him busy.

It's hard not to keep checking the time. Obsessively. By seven p.m. we're still in Utah, when I really want to be running into the convention hotel, making straight for wherever Corbin Bleu is trapped behind a signing table.

"We'll make it," Kourtney tells me in a low voice, so Ricky can't hear. But she needn't worry. Whenever I turn around, he has his headphones on and is singing along in a soft voice. "One more hour, maybe ninety minutes, and we'll be there. The final evening sessions don't even start until nine. When we arrive, I'll distract Ricky, and you get out of this van and GO."

Okay. Sounds like a plan.

Everyone has moved beyond excited to just tense and antsy. We've eaten most of the snacks. We've practiced our medley for the charity performance next week—so many times we've practically strained our voices. Outside, as predicted by Mr. Mazzara and confirmed by Natalie, snow is falling, smearing the windows with icy crystals. Miss Jenn is driving carefully, unlike some of the cars and trucks speeding by on the interstate, splattering the van. Some go by so fast, we get blasted by their gusts of wind, the van shuddering with every blow.

"Don't worry, people," Miss Jenn tells us. The wipers are on high speed. "Slow but steady wins the race. Another ninety minutes and we'll be there."

We all want to believe her, but I think Miss Jenn might be doing some of her magical thinking rather than telling us the truth. I sit fidgeting, doing calculations in my head. If we arrive by nine, or even nine thirty, we're still okay. I don't need to get a place in a workshop. I just need to find the signing table.

We all go quiet for a while. We don't want to distract Miss Jenn on such a slippery road. It's dark now and the snow seems to be getting heavier. I start to worry a little about E.J., but I know he's a good driver and has snow tires on his car. There's no point in texting him, because he always turns his cell phone off when he's driving so he won't be tempted to answer it. And he won't be pulling over for any Insta moments—not when it's this wet and dark.

"Everyone fine back there?" calls Miss Jenn, and we all chorus back yes. Carlos seems to be napping. Ashlyn is palming her new lucky crystals. (She gave her old ones to Miss Jenn.) Ricky is rummaging around in his bag for more snacks. We haven't taken our one planned bathroom break. I think we all just want to get there already.

"Oh," Miss Jenn says. "Oh! Oh! What's happening?"

The van is slowing down to a crawl.

"Why are you braking?" Natalie asks.

"I'm not. Really, I'm not." Miss Jenn sounds panicked. "Hang tight, everyone. We're pulling over."

It's not so much pulling over as creeping over. The van makes puttering sounds, and before Miss Jenn turns off the engine, the engine seems to have turned itself off. Cars zoom past, tires hissing on the wet road. But we're not going anywhere.

"No!" I say, not meaning for it to be out loud. We

need to be driving. We need to get to the convention. But a sinking feeling in my stomach tells me that we're making a pit stop, whether we want to or not.

The van has broken down.

CHAPTER TWELVE

ASHLYN

So much for my new lucky crystals. My old ones never let me down. I'm beginning to think they're just some pretty rocks.

The bad news: It's snowing and we've broken down, somewhere near the Idaho state line. All the snacks are gone. And did I mention *it's snowing*???

Even worse news: With every passing minute, we realize we might not make it in time for the convention tonight. Well, I realize it. Other people are in complete denial. Carlos keeps saying we'll make it because the theater gods will smile on us. Maybe they're laughing at us rather than smiling right now.

The good news: Um . . . there must be something. Actually, there is. The van managed to break down near a rest stop—not the kind with a gas station and somewhere to eat, but a small one with cement restrooms and a scattering of picnic tables. There's a vending machine as well, but it's out of order. No other cars of any kind, but at least we could roll the van off the highway and be sheltered from passing juggernauts.

Generally, I'm a positive person who likes to see the best in people and situations. The opportunities and not the obstacles, as my dad always says. But it's hard to see much good in this. Miss Jenn has called for roadside assistance, and someone is coming. Eventually. Later. Soon but not too soon, apparently.

"They said it's a busy night for call-outs," Miss Jenn tells us. "As if we couldn't guess."

She looks the most devastated of us all, and I feel so bad for her. This trip means as much to her as it does to us. More, perhaps.

Then she asks Ricky to try again with the vending machine, just in case he can magic it into working.

We all venture out to use the facilities, but it's too cold and miserable to stay out long. At least the van is warm-ish. The longer we're stuck here, the colder it's going to get. We might all have to huddle together and wrap ourselves in costumes.

Miss Jenn asks us not to call or text our parents,

because they're sure to get worried and drive out to rescue us. By the time anyone arrives, we'll be on our way. She's trying to sound cheerful, but her face gives her away. I have a sinking feeling we're going to be sitting here for a long time.

I try calling E.J. in case he's close by. At the very least he could buy some food and deliver it to us. Maybe, just maybe, he's a mechanical whizz who can look at the van and know how to fix it. But he doesn't pick up or answer my texts. Reception isn't great out here, and I know E.J. would never text and drive.

"If we can't call our parents because they're too far away to come rescue us," Natalie says, "could you call some of your *HSM* friends going to the convention, Miss Jenn? Maybe one of them is close by."

"Why, sure. Why not?" Miss Jenn doesn't sound very sure. "I don't know that I have up-to-date numbers for . . . some people. And I don't want to bother anyone headed to Jackson. Not with all this snow and whatnot. And they're actors and singers, not mechanics."

There's nothing we can do but wait for the AAA guy.

"They might have some food," says Ricky. He didn't have any luck fixing the vending machine.

"All right, people," says Miss Jenn, in her brightest

voice. "Let's rally the provisions! Anyone who still has food, bring it out."

Gina and I rummage around, as does everyone else. I have an apple, Gina has a bag of mixed nuts, and Ricky discovers his father has snuck some candy bars into his guitar case. Natalie, super organized as ever, gathers up all the provisions and starts working out rations. Really, I think we'll be fine.

But nine o'clock comes and goes and we're still stranded at the rest stop. There's no way we'll make it to the convention tonight. The snow has stopped, and Nini remembered a bag of Doritos in her duffel, so it's not all doom and gloom. But I'm clutching at straws here. Everyone is low. Nini looks close to tears.

Sitting around like this gives me too much time to obsess over that weird text from Big Red. *Hey.* That was it. I replied, but he didn't. At school the next day I heard he couldn't come on this trip. Why didn't he just tell me himself?

Gina is yawning. The battery in Miss Jenn's phone has died. We're all wearing our coats, which makes the van feel even more crowded and stuffy. This isn't a great start to the Best Weekend Ever. Someone's muttering about what will happen if we have to stay out here all night, and I swear I hear someone crying in the back.

"Okay, everyone." Kourtney is on her feet. "You know what'll make us feel better? Singing the holiday medley. We'll give it all we got, and maybe it'll send positive waves out into the universe."

"Great idea." Miss Jenn claps her hands, but she's wearing mittens, so the sound is muted. "Positive waves. Good vibrations. We'll summon our roadside assistance with song!"

Not everyone is quite as enthusiastic at first, but Carlos makes everyone laugh by shouting, "This is life, not a rehearsal!" We're midway through when not one but two sets of lights appear, turning off the highway. One is a tow truck headed our way, and we start cheering as though it's homecoming. The other is a car that parks over by the restrooms.

Almost everyone piles out of the van to see what the verdict is about the engine. Almost everyone gets back in again because it's freezing outside. Miss Jenn is out there, stamping her feet and talking to the mechanic, and then leans in the door.

"Everything's going to be okay," she tells us. "It's just something to do with . . . antifreeze or oil or gas or something. I wasn't really listening. It won't take much longer and then we can hit the road again. We'll get there!"

This is a relief. Sure, we've missed all of tonight's workshops and meet-and-greets. We've missed priority registration for tomorrow's events. Still, we can be there first thing in the morning, lining up for registration. We can get there super early. I don't need to sleep that much.

"The main thing," Gina tells me, "is that you get into the songwriting workshop. And it's not until tomorrow."

Nini has switched seats so she's sitting next to Ricky. They're laughing about something. Everyone seems to be cheering up.

"So how about the rest of that song?" Miss Jenn asks.

"From the top!" shouts Carlos, and we all sing as loud as we can—so loud we're laughing. It's not our best performance, but we're giving it our all.

As we're singing, I wipe a frosty patch of the window clear. The guy from the other car pauses on his way back to his vehicle and turns around. He's all bundled up in a coat and scarf and beanie. He's probably wondering why such loud singing is coming from a high school van.

He walks toward us, arms folded against the cold. We've got a fan! After all, this is our first out-of-school performance. We're almost in another state; this could be a national tour!

He wanders even closer, peering at our van. We're all glowing with the lights from the roadside-assistance truck. When we finish the song, he gives us a thumbs-up.

"The real East High?" he calls to Miss Jenn.

"The one and only," she calls back. "On our way to a convention."

He ambles back to his car and opens the door.

"See you there!" he shouts, and gives us all a wave. Miss Jenn stands watching him drive away, like Elsa from *Frozen* has cast a spell on her.

"Guys, I don't want to be overdramatic or anything," Carlos says, "but I could swear that our audience of one was Lucas Grabeel."

Snow starts falling again, and the car is long gone, but Miss Jenn doesn't move. The guy with the tow truck has to shake her by the shoulder to get her to sign the paperwork. She clambers back into the van, shaking snowflakes off her hair.

"Best. Breakdown. Ever!" she says, and starts the engine.

Insta Interlude

E.J. here, coming right at you from Wyoming.

Little-known fact: Wyoming is the last state alphabetically. Another one of those tomorrow.

I've stopped for one final quick break on my way to the *High School Musical* convention. Hence the terrible lighting. Sorry. Between the snow outside and the fluorescent overheads in here, it's not exactly Insta-worthy.

Anyway, I had a lot of time on the drive to do some thinking. I've realized a few things on the way here. Home truths. Out-of-state truths at this point, but you know what I'm saying.

Sometimes I hear people talk about going on a journey somewhere to "find themselves." I've never really got that, because I've never felt lost. But there's something about traveling alone that makes me wonder. Maybe at #HSMCon I should just do whatever. Not make a plan, not get my heart set on particular workshops or panels. Maybe I should just go with the flow, walk into anything that's open and throw myself into the unknown. See what happens.

Maybe I need to get lost.

But not on the drive there (thanks, GPS).

E.J. out.

611 likes

Add a comment...

CHAPTER THIRTEEN

Six Things Miss Jenn Realizes at the Motel, in Random Order

1. The motel is not close to the convention hotel. Not at all. Maybe the phrase "walking distance" means something different in this state. Everyone will need to be driven there in the van, which means wrangling. You don't really *do* wrangling.

2. E.J. Caswell is not here. By the time your phone is plugged in and working again, you discover he's sent a text message: Loving it at convention. Killer program so far! Workshop teacher showed me the dorm. See you in the morning. What? Did the hotel set up a dorm in

a spare conference room to accommodate all the convention-goers?

3. When you try to call E.J., his phone goes straight to voice mail, which means he's either turned it off or is busy talking to his parents and telling them he's completely unsupervised, aside from this phantom "workshop teacher." Oh well, at least one student managed to get to Friday-night sessions.

4. All the girls squeeze into two rooms; the boys are in one room. You could be the bigger person and ask one or two of the girls to share your room, so there are more bathrooms to go around, and everyone has more space. But you're not the bigger person. You're an exhausted, overexcited, highly artistic person who thinks she may have seen Lucas Grabeel at an interstate rest stop. You need your own room.

5. Tomorrow is going to be one of the defining days of your life and entire professional career. This intermission in your life has gone on long enough. If there's one thing that *HSM* has taught

you, it's to aim high and dream big. (Also: Try not to get cut out of scenes.) Something tells you that this weekend will be a turning point. At last your small part in *HSM* will pay off— not in money, but in making something big and positive and groundbreaking at East High. The stars are aligned. Literally.

6. You may not be emotionally prepared for it, and the van/weather may be conspiring against you, but too bad. The show must go on.

CHAPTER FOURTEEN

CARLOS

Okay. We're in the right state. It's still Friday—just. Apparently the convention hotel where we'll spend all day tomorrow is a short drive away, according to Natalie's recon. And Ricky and I are the only boys on the trip right now. Big Red had to work and Seb had to stay at the farm. Miss Jenn says E.J. is at the convention hotel (after attending a zillion workshops already), and might stay there overnight. So we get a big bed each. If and when E.J. shows up, he has to sleep on the cot. The girls are having a pj party in their two rooms. Ashlyn texted me: LOL we have an interconnecting door!

Great for them. In the boys' room it's lower energy. Neither Ricky nor I are up for much after the long ride. I mean, we did raid the vending machine out by the stairs, and had a mini celebration because this one actually worked and had good snacks. I filled the ice bucket, just out of habit. (I like to pretend I'm backstage in my Broadway dressing room, and someone is about to deliver three dozen roses and a magnum of champagne.) But when I said we're in the right state, I meant Wyoming, not state of mind.

I like Ricky, but he and I are SO different. His accessory of choice is a skateboard. He wears white socks. He's come away for the weekend without any hair gel or a shirt that buttons. But we're friends, and he's not a bad roommate. He doesn't spend all his time flicking from station to station on the TV. After we settle in, he's busy texting Nini and planning to hang out with her before we all go to sleep.

Unfortunately, this motel is one of those open-to-the-lot places where all the communal areas are outside and slick with ice, a frigid wind blowing in from the prairies or the mountains or whatever geographic feature doesn't exist in New York, my spiritual home. Ricky pulls on his coat and wraps a scarf around his neck. He'll brave any weather for Nini.

Once he's gone, I try to video chat with Seb. Our connection is spotty, so his adorable face keeps freezing and pixelating. It's like trying to talk to a jigsaw puzzle.

"Hey!" he says. "So relieved you blooaaaarb . . ."

"What? You're cutting out?"

Silence. Seb's face is frozen with his mouth open.

"Seb?"

"What? Can you hear me now?"

"Yes! Good. You were—"

"—your trip there. Sorry. You go first."

"No, you. Go first. Go on."

Frozen.

"Let me try outside," I say, and make my way through the room, grabbing my jacket. Before I reach the door, Ricky opens it, stamping his feet, his cheeks red.

"Cold out there," he tells me, but I go anyway. He's right. In the parking lot it's frigid, wind swirling snow around. Some of the girls have pasted a glitter star on their front door. The Wildcats pennant has fallen off our van. Symbolic?

"—snow out there," says Seb, or at least that's what I think he says.

"The cold never bothered me anyway," I joke, knowing Seb will get the reference. No response. This is so frustrating. How do people manage long-distance relationships? Why does technology insist on betraying us?

A door bursts open and some of the girls run out, shrieking when the cold air hits them, scampering away in the direction of the vending machine. The sky's so cloudy I can't see any stars. The mountains around us are invisible in the dark. We could be anywhere. This isn't exactly living the dream.

"—cows tomorrow," Seb is saying. "We have to get to the stockyards by eight."

"In the morning?" I squawk. That whole part of Seb's life, with his family and the farm and— What's it called? Animal *husbandry*? It must be so hard for Seb, to go from being Sharpay in *High School Musical* one minute to Curly from *Oklahoma* the next. I really miss him.

Meanwhile Seb is cutting out again, his handsome face distorting on my phone screen. I think he's saying he has to go.

"—up really early and . . ."

"No, no—I get it. We have to be up early as well. I think the first workshops start at nine, and before that it's registration and so on. Also, Miss Jenn said this motel was close to the convention, but I don't think . . . Seb? Are you still there?"

He's gone. Sad, sad, sad. I thought at the very least we'd be able to talk this weekend.

Back in our room, Ricky is sitting up and strumming his guitar.

"Nini and Kourtney were sorting out their clothes

for tomorrow," he says. "I'm going to meet up with Nini later."

He keeps playing. I don't know the song. It sounds melancholy but catchy.

"Is this something you're writing?" I ask him, and he nods.

"Haven't worked out the words yet," he says. "But I think it's going to be called 'Confusion.'"

I lie down on my bed, hands in pockets to warm them up. *Confusion.* That's the word of the day. Why are things harder than they need to be?

Ricky sets his guitar aside.

"I guess I'm too excited about tomorrow to focus," he says. "I can't believe I never used to like musicals. Now I'm like some *HSM* superfan."

"Hey!" I say, hands up like a traffic cop. "Let's not get crazy. You're a newbie, remember."

"Test me," he says, lying back against his pillows, a smug look on his face. "Go on. I bet I can answer any question you throw at me."

"Really?" I like the sound of this challenge. "What's the name of the musical in the movie?"

"*Twinkle Towne.*"

"What does Zeke promise to make for Sharpay?"

"A crème brûlée."

"When Troy says Sharpay is cute, what animal does Chad compare her with?"

"A mountain lion."

I have to admit, he's doing pretty well.

"Troy's father tells him he's not a singer, he's a . . . ?"

"Playmaker. And Troy says he can be both."

"Okay," I say. "One last question."

There's no way he'll get this one. You have to watch the movie at least fifty times to remember this. Which is why I know it by heart.

"When Gabriella corrects her teacher about an equation, she says it should be *what* over pi?"

Ricky pauses. I think I've got him with this one.

"Easy," he says. "Nini's age. Sixteen."

"Not bad," I tell him. Secretly, I'm impressed. He knows a lot more about *HSM* than I thought.

"Do you want to test me on the other two movies?" he asks.

"As if!" I can't believe he's asking this. All that good work just now, and he's blown it.

CHAPTER FIFTEEN

RICKY

Someone raps on our door, and I open it. It's Nini. Her dark eyes look so big; she's like a baby doe, or whatever Bambi is.

"You can come in," Carlos shouts. He's laying out his clothes for tomorrow on his bed and repacking everything else in the most precise way I've ever seen. "Don't freeze to death out there."

"It's okay!" Nini calls back to him. Then she lowers her voice. "Just wanted to say sweet dreams, and see you in the morning."

She stands on her tiptoes to peck me on the cheek. Her lips feel cold. Snow is falling in the lot and the wind is icy. I don't care.

"Let me grab my coat," I say. We can snuggle up together outside. If we stand between our door and the van, we're almost protected. It feels so good to be together, just the two of us.

"I almost feel warm," Nini tells me, cuddling. Our coats are so big and puffy. Hers is white and mine is black. Together we make one giant panda.

"If you'd told me a year ago that I would be this happy about going to a musical-theater convention, I would have laughed."

"So much has happened this year." Nini buries her face in my chest.

"Good, bad, strange," I say. "But now all is good with us. We're together again. That's what matters."

Nini doesn't say anything. She just snuggles in closer, our arms wrapped around each other. From her room we can hear Ashlyn laughing. The other girls' room is even noisier, because they're singing.

Miss Jenn's door opens. She's wearing a big coat over her pj's.

"It's getting late," she says, with an *I'm-sorry* smile. "And cold. Think about your vocal cords!"

"Sorry, Miss Jenn," we chorus.

"We were about to go back to our rooms," Nini tells her.

"When you do, Nini, would you lay down the law with the other girls about quiet time?"

"No problem." Nini starts to pull away from me. I'm not really ready to let her go. But it is getting late. And it is cold. Very, very cold.

Back in our room I stand with the door open for a moment, making sure Nini is back safely.

"Either come in or close the door," complains Carlos. "It's freezing. And snow is getting on my patent leather shoes."

I go to the bathroom to brush my teeth. I haven't talked much to Nini yet about the Big Decision: going to Chicago for the break to be with my mom, or staying in SLC with my dad. If I go, I'll also miss our fundraising performance on Christmas Eve. Nini says she really wants me to be there for that, and so does everyone else. (*We need our Troy!* Miss Jenn told me.) So that's extra pressure to stay home.

When I come out of the bathroom, I see that Carlos has almost finished his repacking. He hums as he gets organized, and I can tell he's in a good mood.

Carlos slithers into bed, his clothes for tomorrow on a chair. By contrast, I find a sock under my pillow and there's a guitar pick stuck in my hair. I knew I shouldn't have tried his hair gel.

Insta Interlude

E.J. here, whispering. I hope you can hear me.

It's not midnight yet, so I can tell you, with 100 percent certainty: This has been the best few hours of my life. And you have to see this. Isn't it the coolest place?

Not literally, of course, because the heating is up really high. This is the convention hotel, and I guess this is one of the bigger conference rooms. The lights in here are low, but I think you can still see the high ceiling and the amazing flower displays.

I did exactly what I said I would: arrived at the convention and walked into the first session I saw. A lot this evening has been about mental preparation, breathing, body awareness, and basic movement. It must be setting us all up for the *HSM*-specific workshops tomorrow. I'm bummed that everyone else is missing this.

This is the last session of the evening. Only about twenty of us are taking part. At first I thought I'd skip it and go to the motel, to hang out with the others, but this is a chance to put my new philosophy into practice. Instead of reaching for the safety of people I know, why not let myself get lost one more time? We'll all be together tomorrow.

So this is my cot, right here, and what I'm wearing are these super-soft white pajamas that were lying on my bed waiting for me. We even have little white slippers. Mine are too little for my feet, but hey, it's the thought that counts.

I'm trying to keep my voice down, because we're supposed to be silent. I helped set up cots for some of the others, who are way older than I expected at an *HSM* con, but that's all good. When they bowed to thank me, I bowed back. One was a woman with hair that's the coolest intense silver. In an earlier session tonight she was my partner in an awareness exercise. We weren't allowed to talk at all apart from this one moment right at the end where we could say one thing to the other person. I had to go first. I said to her, "You make me feel really calm."

She smiled, and said something to me that blew my mind. She said, "You're happiest when you're helping other people on their journeys."

Wow. I'm not sure what she means, but I'm going to think about it. A lot.

A teacher has already come in to let us know—in a whisper—that our breathing exercises and meditations will start soon. She said to take it at our own pace, and sleep whenever we feel the need. I've heard about this kind of advanced theater training. Some of the kids at camp this summer talked about it. You develop better breathing and mindfulness so your singing improves and you can project your voice better.

Someone just shushed me. This is all about inner peace, so I better go before I get into more outer trouble.

E.J. out.

♥ ◯

821 likes

Add a comment...

CHAPTER SIXTEEN

GINA

Before I came to East High, I'd never been invited to a sleepover. When Ashlyn invited me to one at Thanksgiving, it was a first. I was excited, but it didn't happen. Super-sad face, for various reasons. So this road trip is a totally new experience: in a motel in Wyoming. Me, Ashlyn, Nini, and Kourtney sharing two beds, one cot, and one small bathroom. I never thought this would be my idea of a good time, but it is. Even better: I'm here with the theater gang and not back in DC, my alleged new "home."

That call with my mother freaked me out. What if Ashlyn and her family are having second thoughts about me staying with them next semester? They may not want a stranger in their house for so many months. My mom is always big on self-reliance, which is weird in a way, given she works for a federal agency that helps people in time of crisis. She always tells me we have to work hard, take care of ourselves. *Make your own happiness*, Mom says.

Okay, okay, I get it. But sometimes it feels like a lot of pressure. How can I "make my own happiness" when so often that's out of my control? Winning makes me happy, but I'm a performer, not an athlete. There's no tape we run toward and break, with a clear winner and loser. We audition, and other people decide. Power is not in our hands.

I mean, I used to obsess over why I didn't get cast in the role of Gabriella this semester. I felt powerless. I lay awake at night knowing that I was a better dancer than Nini, by about 1,000 percent. I thought: *I've got a bigger singing voice. I've got more experience on the stage.*

But now I think that when Miss Jenn and Carlos cast her in the role of Gabriella, it wasn't a bad thing for me. At first I felt like it was the end of the world. I wasted a lot of time and energy trying to get Nini to step aside. Eventually I realized that being part of the group and playing my own role to make everyone a success was the important thing. Sometimes a star doesn't have to lead the way—it just has to light up the darkness, wherever that darkness exists. Including the back of the stage.

But my main issue right now is just enjoying being a student, having friends, hanging out. It's so hard when I have to move schools every time my mother gets a new work assignment.

I really, really want to stay at East High for another semester. This is the first group where I've really felt I belong, and where I've felt accepted. Now is not the time to go on the road again. Staying at Ashlyn's is my only chance. I hope Ashlyn's mother and my mother agree.

Nini is in the shower, and Kourtney is next door with the other girls, helping them sort out what they're going to wear tomorrow. Ashlyn and I do some stretches on the floor, trying to ignore the stains on the carpet. This motel isn't exactly the convention hotel, where—rumor has it—E.J. made it in time for every possible workshop and has scored himself a room, or a bed, at least. We stretch and twist, and take turns spotting each other with curls.

"The thing is," Ashlyn says, though we haven't been talking much, "I haven't had another text from Big Red. All I got was that one I told you about, where all he said was 'Hey.' I mean, what does that even mean?"

"Sounds like he's trying to start a conversation," I suggest, reaching for my toes. I don't really know. I don't have much experience in this area.

"That's why I replied," she says. "You know, just

saying 'hey' back, and saying I was looking forward to this weekend. But then he avoids me at school and I find out from Ricky that he's not coming on the trip at all."

"That's kinda rude."

"I know he had to work. Maybe he was really bummed about it, and that's why he didn't reply."

It's strange, in a good way, to have a conversation like this with Ashlyn. She's confiding in me, and I'm doing my best to be helpful. I know this is what BFFs do. I see Nini and Kourtney deep in conversation all the time, just like I've seen girls at all the other schools I've attended. Discussing things. Giving each other advice. Listening to each other's problems and working things out. I've never really had that opportunity before. I'm never in one place long enough to establish real friendships, so I've always felt like I'm on the outside.

And the truth is, I don't really know what to say to Ashlyn. Is Big Red just bummed and/or busy? I have no idea.

"What do you think?" Ashlyn asks me. "Do you think I should send another text?"

"Well," I say, "I'm not sure."

"I bet you've dated way more boys than I have," Ashlyn says with a sigh.

I smile and shrug. Part of me wants to tell her that

I've only ever had a handful of random dates, and boys are generally too scared of me to ever text me. This semester I had to *ask* a guy to go to the dance with me, and that was E.J., not a romantic interest at all.

"The thing is with guys . . ." I say, trying to sound knowledgeable. *This is a part you're playing,* I tell myself. *Pretend you're auditioning for the role of BFF and have to improvise some lines.* "The thing is, you can't be the one who looks needy and desperate."

"No! I don't want to seem desperate." Ashlyn looks horrified.

"You've already replied to his text," I continue. "In my experience, boys like you to play hard to get."

This is a lie. I have no experience, not really. The last guy who texted me a *Hey* had me confused with someone else.

"Really?" Ashlyn doesn't seem convinced. "I wouldn't have thought that was Big Red's kind of thing."

"Oh, I'm sure it is." I have to go all out here. "He may seem cute and friendly and all, but I know guys. He texts you, you text him back, he goes silent. The worst thing you could do right now is reach out again. All you're telling him by texting again is *I'm crazy about you.*"

"Eek! I don't want to communicate that," says Ashlyn,

getting up and dusting her hands clean. "I mean, I like him, and we did kiss, but this isn't exactly *West Side Story.*"

I played Maria in a production of *West Side Story* two schools ago, even though I was the youngest girl to audition for the role, but this doesn't seem like the time to boast about it. The other girls in the cast would barely speak to me. This is why I can't do the BFF stuff without making things up and lying about my own life. Ashlyn can't find out I've always been an outcast.

"If I were you," I tell her, "I wouldn't text Big Red again until he contacts you. It's his turn, right?"

"I guess so."

"And even then, you don't have to reply immediately. You need to make boys chase you." I think I saw this on a TV show once. No idea which one. It sounds good, doesn't it? "Make him do the running. Because you're worth it."

Okay—I think that's from a commercial for shampoo or something. But Ashlyn doesn't seem to notice.

"If that's what you think. I guess it makes sense. I'm just such a novice with all this." She stretches and yawns. We can hear the girls in the next room singing "Get'cha Head in the Game." Either they're shouting it or these walls are paper thin.

"Just hold your fire. Let him run after you. We're going to have a great time tomorrow, aren't we?"

Ashlyn smiles. "It would have been fun if he was here as well. He's a pretty good dancer, you know."

I roll my eyes, and she throws a pillow at me. I throw the pillow back. It smacks against the flocked wallpaper behind the bed, narrowly missing the big picture of a bison.

My first-ever pillow fight. This is fun.

CHAPTER SEVENTEEN

KOURTNEY

Our motel room is full. Nini and I are sharing one bed, Ashlyn is in the other bed, and Gina is on the cot. The boys are lucky: They have a whole room for only two people, now that E.J. is staying in the convention hotel overnight.

There are four girls in the room next door as well. They're the ones who've put the glitter star on their door, to make it seem like a star's dressing room. I'm down with that. Though I probably wouldn't have chosen pink glitter.

Snow is really falling outside now, and I'm super relieved we managed to get here despite the weather and the van breaking down. I use the interconnecting door to get back from the next room just as Nini emerges from her shower, wet hair wrapped in a towel.

"Look at the snow!" Ashlyn says, drawing the curtains back on our one window so we can see. "Snow angels, anyone?"

"Sure." Gina gets up from the cot and starts pulling on her coat. "Why not?"

"Wet hair," says Nini, pointing to her towel turban. "And Miss Jenn said we should all be going to bed."

"We won't be long," Ashlyn promises. "And we'll be super quiet."

"My turn for the shower," I say. "Enjoy yourselves getting cold and wet."

"You may be cold and wet as well," Nini tells me in a low voice. "There's not much hot water left."

Trust me to be last in line. At least we only have one night in this motel. Tomorrow night we'll be breaking down again on the interstate on the way back. I can't even believe we're actually going to be at the *HSM* convention tomorrow. Maybe if we were at the hotel, we'd see the signs and start feeling the atmosphere, but at this motel we could be anywhere. Anywhere kind of sad, that is.

I leave Nini to comb her hair out and listen to the shrieks from outside. The shower may be lukewarm and the towels in here may be the consistency of thin sandpaper, but it feels good to get clean after sitting in that stuffy van for so many hours. In the morning there won't be time for much except grabbing a microwaved pastry and watered-down juice in the motel lobby, then heading to the convention hotel. Miss Jenn says we have to take all our things with us, because we'll leave for home straight from the convention.

Tomorrow I'm thinking—still thinking, still considering—about going to the beginners' vocal workshop. Nini has really encouraged me and so has Miss Jenn, but I'm still not sure. The other kids attending this convention are all going to be stars at their own high schools. Some of them might go to fancy performing arts schools, like the one in Denver where Nini has been offered a (top secret!) place. Some people here may even be adults who are *HSM* superfans and maybe even musical theater professionals. Their idea of a "beginner" and mine might be really different.

And then there's me. A church singer, not a stage singer. The backstage maven who does the best makeup anywhere in Mountain Standard Time. But I've never had a real role in a production, let alone a single singing lesson.

One other place I like to sing, aside from church: the shower. One of my favorite songs to belt out is "Walk Away" from *High School Musical 3: Senior Year.* I don't care what Carlos says: I love that movie.

I may be going nuts from too much time in that van, but I swear I can hear my own backup singers echoing the "Walk Away" line before I soar back in. Is this what happens to everyone who watches a movie or sings a song too often? We start hearing backup singers and orchestration?

When I come out from the bathroom, I realize that it was Nini singing along. She must have heard me through these cardboard walls.

"You sound fantastic," she says. "I'm serious. You have an amazing voice. You really need to go to that vocal workshop in the morning, and make sure someone important hears you. Hearing you sing makes me feel warm and happy and exhilarated. It makes me want to write a song for you!"

"Okay—thanks." It's weird. I feel myself blushing. Why? Embarrassment is not a Standard Kourtney Emotion.

"Really," says Nini. "You rock. I can't wait for you to take part in a workshop where other people will tell you the exact same thing."

I've been getting used to the idea that I could take

part in the spring musical. I talked it over with Nini, and I know Miss Jenn wants me to audition.

Nini is so supportive and encouraging. I'm lucky to have her in my corner. But if I get this embarrassed with Nini overhearing me in the shower, I'm clearly not ready to be a serious contender on the stage. A real performer has the courage to get out there and dare to fail. I can't even dare to succeed.

I go back to the bathroom and prepare my hair for bed. In the mirror my face is clean, without a scrap of makeup. I stand there brushing my teeth, looking at the real me. The Kourtney everyone knows at school has swagger. She's bold and sassy, and nobody makes a fool of her.

But this Kourtney, singing on the stage? She's vulnerable. She wants something and she's not sure if she can get it. It's not just a question of stage fright. I'm used to singing in a choir or singing backup in big numbers. But when I sing alone, I feel like my inner self is on show. It's exposing. My usual deal is makeup and costumes, and when you think about it, that's all about disguise. Artifice. Looking better or different or more extreme. Not about your raw, real self. Your raw, real emotions. I'm afraid I'll sing too loud, and show too much.

Making the outside of things look good—that's easy.

Revealing what's inside of you—much scarier. I'm not used to feeling scared of things, but I guess this is what I'm feeling right now. Afraid.

If my name gets called tomorrow, and I have to step up in front of strangers and sing, what if I choke?

CHAPTER EIGHTEEN

[Mis]Communication Recap: Friday-Night Edition

BIG RED

My Friday-night shift is almost over. It's been busy, but I've still managed to check my phone about a hundred times. Ashlyn's been posting on Instagram: with Gina in the van; with Gina bouncing on a bed in their motel room; with Nini outside a motel room door, pointing to a glitter star someone's stuck there. A group shot outside a vending machine, with everyone except E.J. and Miss Jenn.

But Ashlyn hasn't sent any texts to me. Not one. Is this because it's my turn? When I didn't reply to her text on Wednesday night, it's because I didn't want to admit I couldn't go on the trip with everyone else this weekend. I was so bummed about it.

Maybe I should have talked to her in school the next day, but I had two tests and needed to spend lunchtime working on the History assignment. On Friday everyone on the trip was so happy and excited that I felt even worse about not going. I just kept to myself. Laid really low.

Was that the wrong thing to do? I have no idea what girls expect. Maybe I've been cowardly, and I should have sent her a reply. But by Thursday it was already too late.

This feels like a social minefield. I know all about minefields in video games, but that's different. You get blown up in a game, you close out and play again tomorrow. Things don't work that way in real life, with real people. With real girls. At real schools.

Okay. They're all still awake at their motel, I'm sure. I'll send a text right now to Ashlyn, just casual, as though I'm checking in. Then it'll be her turn and I'll be off the hook. I think. This is *so* complicated.

Hey—again.

That's it. That's my text. I press Send before I can overthink it. Can't have a repeat of Wednesday night. Hopefully she'll read it and reply, and then I can reply, and then we'll be having a conversation.

My shift ends and my dad and I drive home. No reply

from Ashlyn. Check again. No reply. No reply. No reply. No reply.

Get ready for bed, extra slow. No reply. No reply. Maybe they don't have reception up there in Jackson Hole? Nope. Another Insta post of Gina and Ashlyn making snow angels in the motel parking lot. #EastHighExcitement. And Ricky has texted me three times since they arrived.

So Ashlyn is just choosing not to text me back. It's what I deserve, I guess, for leaving it too long. Maybe I have to step up now. Say something more than *Hey*.

I text again.

Looks like you're all having a good time.

No reply. No reply. No reply. I have to get some sleep. It would be so much easier if I was there. Better to read people in person than try to read between the lines, or lack of them. What's really going on?

CHAPTER NINETEEN

[Mis]Communication Recap: Friday-Night Edition

ASHLYN

After nothing from Big Red for almost two days, I get two texts. I show them both to Gina.

"See?" she says. "Treat 'em mean, keep 'em keen."

"Really? But it seems like he wants to talk. I could just say something about the van ride and the breakdown and—"

Gina shakes her head. "Let him wait. He made you wait, didn't he? This is a game, Ash. Boys like playing games. And, this time, you get to be the player as well."

"I don't like playing these kind of games," I say.

"Shh, you two," Kourtney says. "We have to get up in, like, four hours."

"Sorry, Kourt," I say. She's right. Time for lights-out.

That doesn't stop me from snuggling down under the covers and looking at my phone again. The light won't bother anyone if I keep the phone low.

Gina probably has more experience than I do with guys. But it feels strange to me to play games with another person, especially when that person is a good guy like Big Red. I mean, I think he's a good guy. He *seems* like a good guy, not some kind of player. Maybe I'm not a great judge of character. For most of this semester I thought Gina was aloof and mean, and she's turned out to be a friend.

I type: Trip was long but excited about tomorrow. Sorry you're not here.

My finger hovers. Shall I send this? Why not? It's friendly. It's polite. I hate ignoring people for no good reason.

No. Gina's right. I have to stay strong. He made me wait, so I can make him wait. I'll text him tomorrow. Yes, that's exactly what I should do.

Delete.

CHAPTER TWENTY

[Mis]Communication Recap: Friday-Night Edition

MISS JENN

Benjamin Mazzara:

Did you arrive safely in WY? Concerned about weather, van, your driving prowess.

Me:

Safe and sound. No issues with driving. None at all. Thanx for yr faux concern.

Benjamin Mazzara:

Not faux. Genuine.

Me:

OK. Thanx.

Benjamin Mazzara:

Good rooms at convention hotel? Attended a
STEM symposium there once and found the
conference facilities excellent.

Me:

No room at hotel. We're at motel nearby. Not
nearby enough. Outskirts. Maybe not even WY.

Benjamin Mazzara:

Keep your spirits up. I always admire your pluck,
if not your planning.

Me:

Kind of you to say that. I think.

Benjamin Mazzara:

Make sure to bring the van back in good
condition.

Me:

LOL

Benjamin Mazzara:

You forgot the period after "LOL."

Me:

Good night Mr. M. Note the period.

Benjamin Mazzara:

Duly noted. Good night, Miss Jenn. And good
luck.

Insta Interlude

E.J. here. Early Saturday. Sun's up, and the snow's stopped. It's going to be an amazing day.

I'm so glad I drove here alone and arrived in time for the Friday-night workshops. They were so worth it.

I know I'm recording this super early, and most of you are probably still in bed. But I've already had a breakfast of organic cereals, local winter fruits, and coffee ethically grown in Namibia. Some of the others were making green smoothies in a blender, which FYI was not silent at all, and unfortunately the lid wasn't on right. So we all ended up wearing the smoothie on our faces, hair, clothes, shoes. I drank a glass as well, after licking some off my face. It looked disgusting but tasted okay. I don't know what was in it exactly, but soap and water don't seem to be moving it much. Hopefully the health benefits extend to skin care.

I saw the signs for #HSMCon registration for today's events, but the desk doesn't open until eight. So in the meantime—after trying to wash off some of the green splatter—I decided to squeeze in another pre-workshop. Sticking to my resolution of getting lost and being present in the moment.

The teacher announced this class was called "Theater of the Unheard." Weird, but I went along with it. She led us in a series of dance movements around the room, without saying a single word. We had to mimic her. Flying like a bird, plodding through mud, acting like waves in the ocean. I loved it, I have to say. It was a great warm-up for whatever else happens today.

One thing I wasn't expecting: All the other convention people are really much older. But maybe that's because the movies came out years ago? I'm the youngest by at least ten years. I thought it would be mostly high school kids and young people here. Who knew?

I haven't seen any of the others yet. A line is

already forming outside for registration. Maybe I can sneak the East High crew in so they don't have to freeze out there. Time to try, once again, to clean the green off my Wildcats basketball uniform, and get ready to rock today's sessions.

E.J. out.

934 likes

Add a comment...

Skip breakfast. Dress warm. We're Just Getting Started.

#HSMCon update: Beginners vocal workshop full. But you are [still] the music in me: sign up for Advanced!

I Don't Dance? You will in our Cafeteria Choreography class. Almost full: arrive early #HSMCon

Update #HSMCon: Industry panel SRO. Get'cha head in the game if you don't want to miss out.

Bet on it: our HSM stars here AM only. Arrive early to join the signing lines #HSMCon

Want it all? Arrive early. Only five places left in the songwriting class #HSMCon

CHAPTER TWENTY-ONE

Miss Jenn's Notes to Self re:
Activities on Saturday a.m.,
Almost All Unplanned

1. Alarm at six, and everyone up! Everything looks brighter in the morning. That could be because of all the glistening snow, like the snow that's piled window-high around the van, but don't let it discourage you. Everyone is buzzing and zinging and other words with a z in them, apart from the people who are moaning about how dark and/or cold it is, and how their costumes are not made of wool. Sure, you have to borrow a shovel from the motel and take turns clearing snow away from the van. Sure, you have to try to cram everyone's bags back in when those bags seem to have trebled in size overnight.

Sure, you have a longer-than-ideal drive ahead on icy roads and then a massive line to get into the convention itself. Oh well! What time is it? Convention time!

2. Don't freak out when everyone starts reading #HSMCon alerts from their phones. Some workshops are already full. It's standing-room-only ALREADY at the industry panel. Lines are long. You need to be strong. Time for some magical thinking.

3. In the van, lead everyone in vocal exercises to get the blood pumping! Tell them they got this! Pray the van starts. Kind of wish you'd accepted Mr. Mazzara's offer to drive up and help you out. Kind of wish you were in your own little car and not trying to be responsible and drive teenaged people around. Feel selfish for even thinking that. Could this be because you're a millennial?

4. When you discover the convention hotel is really a convention *complex*, don't panic. Find the right building with its massive *High School Musical*

banners and even more massive, snaking, out-of-control, million-mile-long line of excited young people. This is not what Mr. Mazzara would refer to as a "professional learning environment" but whatever. Drop everyone off. Tell them to save you a place. Then spend the next twenty minutes looking for somewhere to park. You may as well have walked from the motel.

5. Ignore the fact that all the transfer stickers the kids made for the sides and back of the van are peeling off or frozen over. Also ignore the fact that every second school van you see has done the same thing, so all the vans look identical and your Unique Selling Point as The Real Thing doesn't seem quite so USP-ish anymore.

6. Text E.J. to ask if he's already in line or if he's made it inside. Knowing him, he's already signed up for the day's workshops and panels, and is at some breakfast buffet with Ashley Tisdale. Maybe he can save you a seat at the industry panel? You have to get into that. YOU HAVE TO GET INTO THAT.

CHAPTER TWENTY-TWO

[Mis]Communication Recap: Saturday-Morning Edition

E.J.

Miss Jenn:

E.J., have you registered already?

E.J.:

Just finished a workshop.

Miss Jenn:

What????

E.J.:

A warm-up workshop.

Miss Jenn:

Saturday program doesn't start for another 90
minutes. Where are you????

E.J.:

In the hotel. About to head to the registration
desk. Where are you?

Miss Jenn:

In line behind c 100 people. What was this
pre-workshop?

E.J.:

Theater of the Unheard.

Miss Jenn:

???

E.J.:

Hang on. Just reading signs.

E.J.:

Now I get it. There are two conventions going on
at this hotel.

Miss Jenn:

What's the other convention?

E.J.:

Mindfulness and Meditation.

E.J.:

No wonder we had to be silent the whole time.

E.J.:

C U in line.

CHAPTER TWENTY-THREE

RICKY

I had no idea there would be hundreds of people in this line. And if I thought that *we* were pumped up in the van, then everyone else must have been drinking soda and eating donuts for the last five hours straight, because they seem on the edge of hysteria.

Also, practically everyone is wearing red East High gear from the movies, which is weird, as we actually go to East High, and our school colors are red, white, and blue. But we're wearing red, too, of course, because we're pretending to be at the East High in the movies, rather than East High in real life, where the movies were filmed. Ashlyn likes this meta stuff, but in my opinion it's way too early in the morning for it.

Miss Jenn drives off to find somewhere to park, and we all huddle at the back of the line. It's still really cold, though it's not snowing anymore. The sky is blue and the mountains look pasted against it, white and rugged.

Before Miss Jenn arrives, another fifty people—maybe more—are behind us. I hope we can all fit in the hotel. Everyone else is freaking, too.

"We better not miss out on any workshops because they're all full," Ashlyn says. "I really, really want to get into the songwriting class."

"I'll make sure you do," promises Gina. "Even if I have to mow everyone else down to get them out of your way."

"Guys!" Natalie appears with the updated schedule and site map that were handed out at the door. "Can you believe who's here?"

"Ashley Tisdale?" asks Carlos. I think that's what he says; his voice is muffled because he has a scarf wrapped around his mouth.

"Almost as good," Natalie says. "It's the daughter of the dog who played Sharpay's puppy!"

"Sharpay's shar-pei?" Gina jokes.

"Sharpay's dog was a Yorkie," Carlos tells her, pulling his scarf free. "And I didn't come all the way to this winter wonderland to see one of Santa's *elves*. I want the real thing."

I put my arms around Nini to snuggle with her and keep her warm. Nini's my girl. After the break, we're going to have a great semester at school together, and perform in the spring musical, and nothing—nobody—will come between us ever again.

This morning she's wriggly, like Sharpay's Yorkie puppy.

"Anything up, babe?" I ask her. "Are you cold?"

"Nope!" She beams at me. "Just antsy. Can't wait to get inside and . . . and *do* stuff."

"Shall we make a plan about workshops?"

"Yeah . . . sure." Again she seems uncertain. Natalie passes around copies of the revised schedule she picked up at the door, and everyone's freaking out about the alerts coming thick and fast from the convention. So many things are already full, or only have a few places left. Seriously, if some people here can't get into Cafeteria Choreography, they may explode.

"How about the duets workshop?" I ask Nini. "It says everyone needs to pair up for that, so—"

"I have something to do in session one," she says in a rush. "A thing with Kourtney."

"It's not until this afternoon," I tell her.

"Oh! Sure. Good. Let's do it."

She seems super distracted. I want to ask her what her thing with Kourtney is, but everyone around us is moving.

"Line's moving!" shouts Gina, and we all shuffle forward. After another ten minutes of messing around in line, we're getting closer to the door. There's no sign of Miss Jenn yet.

"She's had to park in the far lot," Carlos reports, practically bouncing with agitated anticipation. He and Miss Jenn are either in touch a lot by phone or he can read her mind. Big Red calls him "Deputy Jenn."

"I wish we'd arrived earlier," Nini says, almost as though she's talking to herself.

"The doors wouldn't have opened any sooner," I tell her, reaching out to pull her close.

"But we would have been farther ahead in the line," she says.

I try to keep her positive. "The first sessions don't start until nine," I point out. "I know some things are filling up, but there are still lots of choices."

"No, there aren't," Kourtney interjects, pacing past with the schedule an inch from her nose. It's not like her to be so negative.

"And the line is moving fast," I say to Nini, though this is a lie. "We have plenty of time to get in and register."

"There are . . . other things to do inside." Nini still won't relax. "You know, we need to get our makeup and costumes on. And there'll be stuff to see. There's an official program we can buy, right?"

"Definitely," Ashlyn tells her. "I just got the alert."

Everyone's phones are beeping. It's earsplitting. Nini shivers.

"Come here if you're cold," I say, opening my arms, and she steps close.

"You know, Ricky," she says, and tilts her beautiful face up. "I wish I could—I wish I could—"

"What?"

She looks wistful. "Nothing. It's just there's a lot to think about right now."

"I know." I pull her close and rest my chin on her head. "But we don't have to think about anything today, do we? Except being here and having fun."

"What? Oh yeah. Right. Good idea. Don't think about anything. Until we get back."

"Nini!" Kourtney's been working the line, and now she's back, clearly bursting to report on what she's seen. They go into a huddle, bent over the program.

"Hey." E.J. appears from nowhere, looking sheepish.

He has something green smeared around his mouth and on his Wildcats jersey as well.

"What's that?" I ask, pointing at his face, and he tries to rub it off with one finger.

"Oh! It's just juice," he tells me. "Well, a kale smoothie with broccoli foam that got all over everyone. Blender eruption. Long story. I've been trying to wash it off all morning."

"Why would you have something so disgusting?" I ask.

"I didn't really have a choice. It was on my face."

I'm not sure when and where this erupting blender incident took place. It's just another strange clue in the Mystery of E.J.

"Where exactly were you last night, man?" I ask him. E.J. looks at the ground, then looks around. Everyone is too busy chattering about the schedule or doing dance moves to notice.

He leans close. "The thing is, I did a stupid thing that turned out to be a great thing."

"What are you talking about?" Everyone is acting weird this morning. Maybe we've gone to Oz instead of Wyoming.

"Last night when I arrived, I went to what I thought was the convention. But it turned out to be another convention. It was about mindfulness and living in the moment."

"What?" This is so crazy.

"But," he says, lowering his voice even more, "I really got a lot out of it. I feel as though I learned something."

"Like, go to the right convention? Don't stand too close to blenders of green liquid?"

"Like, talking doesn't always mean expressing things. Sometimes silence really is golden."

I'm not sure what he's talking about, but I try to roll with it. "So does this mean you're not going to do your Instagram posts anymore?"

E.J. laughs and smacks me on the arm. "Not that. They're already short and to the point. Distilled knowledge. No, I mean . . . in life *generally*. Less is more. Sometimes we say things that don't need to be said. We worry about what we said in the past and what we're going to say in the future. When really we should just be living in the moment. Being mindful. Trusting our instincts. Not stressing so much."

Maybe the cold is getting to me, because what E.J. is saying almost makes sense. I've been doing exactly what he's talking about—worrying about what I'm going to say and going to do. Obsessing over the "right" thing to do about my parents and the holidays isn't helping. I need to trust my instincts. When I know, I'll know.

"That's actually kinda helpful," I tell him. "Maybe we should all skip this convention and go to yours."

E.J. looks doubtful. "Don't get me wrong—it was great," he says. "But there was a total ban there on fried food, and no one was supposed to talk, let alone sing. I think this convention might be more fun."

"If we ever get in," I joke, which causes a major flurry of "No!" and "Don't say that!" from everyone around me.

"They're living in the moment," E.J. tells me, in his most annoying E.J.-knows-best voice. "That's why they're complaining right now. You're harshing their vibe."

"Yeah, stop *harshing our vibe*," Carlos says. I can't tell if he's being sarcastic or not. If I'm trusting my instincts, I guess I would say . . . yes.

CHAPTER TWENTY-FOUR

Freaking Out: Standing-in-Line Edition

CARLOS

So this line is creeping along like an amateur performance of *Cats*, and Miss Jenn is still AWOL. What if we all get in before she arrives? She'd have to go to the back of the line, and that would throw off our entire secret plan of action for the day. Unless she could pull strings. Please may Miss Jenn be able to pull strings. These alerts from the convention are making me very nervous.

To take my mind off the impending disaster, I try to FaceTime Seb again. This is his busy day, or at least morning, but it would be cool to speak, even for just a few minutes. I miss his sweet face. It's hard to watch Nini and Ricky snuggling up and not think that Seb and I could have had an amazing time here together. He could have joined me and Miss Jenn on our mission. With his handsome face, he'd have been able to persuade some *HSM* star to visit our school.

But once again, Seb and I just can't connect. Picture frozen, or words cutting out. Seb is somewhere noisy, so he's trying to shout. I'm somewhere noisy, too, though around me there's more shrieking and singing and around him there are more animal noises. Different worlds. That's how it feels right now. We're out of sync.

It's super frustrating. E.J. walks up, his shirt smeared with green (what?) and puts a hand on my shoulder. I think he's trying to be reassuring.

"Let it go," he says.

"You're quoting *Frozen* now?" I ask. Seb has disappeared altogether. *Failed connection*, my screen reads.

"My mindfulness teacher. From my workshop last night. She says we have to let things go, rather than try to change what we cannot control."

I open my mouth to shoot some sassy retort in his direction, but . . . well, what he says makes sense. Seb and I can't control annoying technology and long-distance hiccups. We can't magic ourselves into the same place today.

"I can't believe I'm saying this," I tell him, "but thanks. That's really not bad advice. And also, why are there grass stains on your shirt?"

E.J. flashes his most enigmatic smile and walks away. I try calling Seb again. *Failed connection.* Sigh.

CHAPTER TWENTY-FIVE

Freaking Out:
Standing-in-Line Edition

KOURTNEY

Okay, so I just got an #HSMCon update on my phone, and it turns out the beginners' vocal workshop is full. Nightmare. Sad face. Massive disappointment. Just last night I was terrified about taking part in it. Now I feel devastated about missing it.

Nini tells me to take the advanced vocal workshop instead. "You can do it, Kourt," she says. "Everyone else here is just another schoolkid. It's not as though they're professionals. You can totally hold your own."

She may be right. Or not. I head off on a surveillance mission, working the line to check out the competition. Not that this is a competition, as such, but I'm not going to be bringing out my raw inner self in a room around kids who've been acting in commercials since they were babies or starred in a regional tour of *Annie.*

I pull my coat tight, because *it is cold,* and go for a wander. I'm listening for other singers waiting to get into the convention. A lot of groups are singing, mainly to keep warm. These kids are all musical theater nerds, and they're doing mini performances—songs, dances, scenes from the movies. I'm looking for something that will tell me *Yes, Kourtney, you should take that advanced vocal workshop and not be afraid.* Or something that will tell me *No, Kourtney, you are way out of your league here. Keep singing at church, and accept that your true talents lie in costume and makeup.*

That's when I realize what I've done. When Miss Jenn dropped us off to get a place in line, I left my big duffel in the van with everyone's luggage. It's got my makeup bag in it. I'm supposed to be doing everyone's makeup when we get inside! All I have on me is some lip gloss. No brushes, no eye shadow palette, no concealer. Disaster!

Nini is running toward me, her face a picture of horror as well.

"Kourt, I just realized," she says, out of breath.

"That I left my makeup in the van? Ahead of you on that one."

"No!" Nini winces. "I didn't even think of that. I was

thinking about our costumes for Gabriella and Taylor. They're still in the van as well."

"No!" I slap my forehead. I spent half an hour ironing them last night. "Your red dress! My purple-tie shirt!"

"We're idiots," groans Nini. "We come all this way and forget the most important things. I've been thinking so much about getting a program and—you know. Getting the signatures for Ricky."

"As soon as we see Miss Jenn, I'll find out where the van is and go find everything."

"But you can't miss the first session," Nini tells me. "You *have* to get into that advanced vocal workshop. I'm serious."

Speaking of Miss Jenn, where is she? We've been in line all this time and no one has seen her. Either she's parking the van in Idaho or she's managed to pull strings to get herself in already. She was in the movie, after all.

E.J. strolls up, beaming, as though he's having the Best Day Ever. Unlike me.

"Um, why is there green stuff on your ear?" I ask him.

"Still? Don't worry about it." We're all freaking out, but E.J. is chill. "You seem stressed."

"Well, yeah. I left my makeup kit in the van, and the outfits Nini and I were planning to wear for the cosplay, and—"

E.J. puts his hands on my shoulders.

"Don't worry," he says. "You guys will shine. It's inside you already. You don't need makeup and costumes for other people to realize you're both stars."

"What?" I ask him. One night of meditating on a cot—so I've heard—and E.J. is like the wise old owl. Except I think the wise old owl talked less.

The bird winks at me and floats away. I'd like to say his advice was helpful. Sensible, yes. But not even wise old E.J. can magic me up my makeup and costumes.

"What time is it? Convention time!" another school group shouts, throwing their cheerleaders high into the air.

Actually, it's freak-out time. Is it too late to go home?

CHAPTER TWENTY-SIX

Freaking Out:
Standing-in-Line Edition

MISS JENN

1. So you may have trouble finding the van later, because it's so far away and all the other vans look the same. You may be illegally parked. You may be sort of in a snow drift. At least the hotel is in sight. The line is immense. You're already behind the curve. Is that a math thing? Ask Mr. Mazzara sometime.

2. At the front of the line there's security (burly) and convention staff (officious). See if you can pull some strings to get your kids in right away. Play the "real East High" card. Play the "I was

in the first movie as a dancer" card. Play the "Is that the last apple?" card, just in case anyone's seen outtakes. When you have no more cards and no more strings, walk away with your head held high, even though other people in line are looking at you with evident disdain/annoyance/nonrecognition. So you have no pride left. That's okay. You're here for the kids. Remember what you told Mr. Mazzara earlier this semester: You believe in them—not because all of them are going to be Broadway stars, but because they won't.

3. Find your gang. Almost all of them seem to be having some personal crisis, emotional turmoil, or explosion of self-doubt. Most of the workshops they were hoping to take are already full. Some of them have left things in the van, and they don't realize that the van is far, far away and possibly lost forever. Smile. Calm everyone down. Tell them the end of the line is in sight, and then the magic will begin. However humiliated, defeated, or frantic you may feel inside, keep it to yourself. Today you want to help make *their* dreams come true.

4. Oh—and tell E.J. to clean that green stuff off his shirt. That kid looks like he fell asleep in a spinach patch. Wildcats wear red!

CHAPTER TWENTY-SEVEN

Freaking Out:
Standing-in-Line Edition

BIG RED

I'm in the line at the grocery store, picking up some milk and bread. It's eight in the morning on a Saturday, and I would much rather be in bed. But my mother panics when there's snow, and thinks we have to get in supplies for a month-long blizzard.

Just as it's almost my turn to pay, I get a text from her. Too late, I want to tell her. I'm not giving up my place in line just to get more cheese slices or something.

But it's good news. Kind of. Someone else can work my shift tonight. In fact, they really want to work the shift because they need the money. Is that okay?

This means I could have gone to the *HSM* convention after all.

"Unbelievable," I say out loud. The guy in front of me gives me a hard look. I guess he thinks I'm complaining about how long he's taking to unload his basket.

This is so frustrating. I could have been on that van yesterday! I text Ricky to tell him, though there's nothing he can do about it. Nothing either of us can do.

He gets back to me right away. Could u get here in time for the afternoon sessions?

In theory, sure. But who's going to drive me five hours to Wyoming? I've missed the bus, literally.

I didn't realize until now how disappointed I was about missing the convention. Things are so bad that all I can send to Ricky is a sad-face emoji. I never use emojis. That's how bad things are.

CHAPTER TWENTY-EIGHT

Freaking Out:
Standing-in-Line Edition

RICKY

E.J. is still working the line, dispensing his newfound wisdom, and wanders up.

"Dude, what's wrong?"

"Nothing." I want to say *And don't call me dude*, but I know he's trying to be helpful. "It's just Big Red could have been here after all. It turns out he doesn't have to work tonight."

"No!" E.J. seems genuinely disappointed. "And there's no way he can get here?"

"Someone would have to drive him. Five hours each way."

"Hasn't he got a million cousins?" E.J. asks. He and Ashlyn have a family like Big Red's—so many cousins they have to have holiday parties at a hotel. "Could one of them drive him right now to Pocatello, Idaho?"

"Why?" I've never heard of the place.

"It's about halfway between SLC and here. Tell him to get dropped off at the Fort Hall gas station at exit ninety-nine on the interstate. I'll be waiting for him."

"Are you for real?" I'm already texting Big Red: Can you get a ride to Pocatello ID?

"If he leaves soon, he can get to Pocatello by ten thirty. We'll be back here just after lunch."

"But you'll miss all the morning sessions," I say, and E.J. shrugs.

"I've already been to, like, five different workshops. Sure, they were at the wrong convention, but I got a lot out of them. Text him. See what he says."

Another ten texts, with pauses so Big Red can talk to his mom. He's at the grocery store, and has to get home. But maybe . . .

My phone dings again.

"Okay!" I tell E.J. "He says if you're serious, his mom will drive him to Pocatello. They're leaving as soon as he gets home, in about ten minutes."

"Tell him I'll be waiting for him in Idaho," says E.J. I kind of want to hug him. But I don't want to get green stuff on my shirt.

"This is really good of you," I tell him. "Really generous."

"Hey," says E.J., flashing me his best Insta smile. "This is what the convention is all about, isn't it? I mean, both conventions. It's about doing the right thing, for yourself and for the team. And anyway, things are way more fun when we're all together. I'd hate for Big Red to miss out on all this."

I give him Big Red's number, and promise to update Miss Jenn.

"Thanks again," I say. "Really."

"E.J. out," he says, and jogs away.

CHAPTER TWENTY-NINE

Freaking Out: Standing-in-Line Edition

ASHLYN

"Hey!" says Ricky as he bounds over to me. I guess *hey* is the word of the week.

"Hello," I reply, but he doesn't seem to notice that I'm annoyed.

"Big Red is on his way. Isn't that great?" Ricky is beaming. "He doesn't have to work tonight after all. He'll be here around lunchtime."

I don't know what to say or how to feel. So I say nothing. I wish I could feel nothing.

"He just texted," Ricky says, brandishing his phone in case I can't make the connection. "Better late than never, right?"

"Sure," I finally manage to say, though I can't manage much enthusiasm. The line surges forward again, and we surge with it. Ricky races back to Nini.

"What was that?" Gina nudges me. "Big Red is coming?"

"Apparently." He hasn't sent me any more texts. I haven't replied to his. Now it feels awkward. I'm kind of glad he'll be here, but what if he's annoyed that I've blown off his messages?

"He hasn't been in touch with you?" Gina asks. She looks guilty. Guilty and cold. The sun may be shining, but it's bitter out here.

I shake my head. "He told Ricky he's on his way. But now I'm wondering— I don't know."

"What?" Gina can't meet my eyes.

"I'm wondering if I should have replied last night. Even if it was just to say 'hey' or something like that. But don't listen to me. I don't know anything about . . . *relationships*. You have way more experience than I do."

Gina hops from foot to foot, staring at the ground.

"It was really good to get your advice," I say. "I so don't know what I'm doing."

"The thing is," Gina says to the sidewalk, "I don't know either."

"What do you mean?" I ask. This is a really different Gina from last night. Then, she was all confident and knowing. Now, she looks as mixed-up as I feel.

"I mean, I don't really have as much experience as I made out. If we're going to be friends—and I really want us to be friends—then I should be honest with you. I heard E.J. talking to Carlos just now, and some of what he was saying really made sense."

"E.J.? You mean, my cousin E.J.? The one who looks like he's been rolling in mown grass?" I love my cousin, but sometimes he does crazy things, and thinks even crazier things, and says the craziest things of all.

Gina laughs, though she's still looking guilty. Maybe even remorseful. "He was saying something about not trying to force things. How we shouldn't try to change what we cannot control."

That's pretty good advice, I have to admit. Where is E.J.?

"So that's why I think I should be honest with you," Gina continues. "I should never have given you that advice last night. I really have no idea what you should do, because I've never had a boyfriend."

"Never?" I can't believe Gina is as naive as I am.

"You know what E.J. was saying to Carlos?" Gina

takes my mittened hands and squeezes them. "He said, *Don't follow other people and what they think you should do. Trust your instincts.*"

Wow. Maybe I should listen to E.J. more often.

"Okay," I tell her. "I guess that's what I should do."

"And don't ask me for relationship advice *ever*," Gina says, smiling. Then she's laughing, as though we're talking about something hilarious.

"What is it?"

"Just something Carlos said, after E.J. gave him all that unsolicited advice. He said he was trying to trust his instincts, but he couldn't hear them over the sound of E.J. talking."

We both burst out laughing, and for a moment the cold doesn't seem quite so cold, and the sky is the happiest shade of blue.

CHAPTER THIRTY

NINI

And we're in!

Every moment in that freezing line was worth it. The convention hotel is festooned with red-and-white banners and life-size cardboard figures of the original cast. The soundtrack is blaring in every corridor, and each room where seminars or workshops are taking place is named after a character—like the Troy Bolton Break-Out Room, or the Sharpay Evans Ballroom.

Kourtney and I may not have our makeup or our cosplay outfits, but that's not important anymore. Not to me, anyway. We're here, and I have a mission. Buy a program, and find as many stars as possible to sign it for Ricky. I might even try to get a paw print from

Sharpay's Yorkie puppy, if that poor pooch isn't completely mobbed.

I know I missed out on a big one last night, because Corbin Bleu is already gone. But according to our #HSMCon alerts, Monique Coleman, who played Taylor, is here this morning. Alyson Reed, who played Ms. Darbus, is here—I have to tell Ashlyn if she doesn't know already. Olesya Rulin is here: she played Kelsi Nielsen. Chris Warren, who played the baking basketballer Zeke Baylor, will be here this afternoon. The rumors that Ashley Tisdale is dropping in have been going up and down the line, but the program will "neither confirm nor deny." Exciting! And of course we're all convinced that Lucas Grabeel will be here, because Miss Jenn says she is 100 percent positive that he was the guy who drove into our breakdown rest stop last night.

Whoever is here: *I will find you, and I will get you to sign the program for Ricky.* He has been so sweet to me this week, and I want to give him the perfect memento of the show that brought us back together. I need something super big and special and romantic to distract him from the revelation that I'm going to the Youth Actors Conservatory in Denver. He still might be upset when I tell him. But at least he'll know how I feel about him, and how happy I am we're back together.

Still, I can't tell him just yet. Not this weekend. I almost blurted it out in the line this morning, because I really hate keeping things from him. But at the last minute I lost my nerve. It would send a giant dark cloud over the convention, and we had enough problems with bad weather last night.

Everyone scatters, racing off to sign up for whatever workshops and panels still have places. We have much less time than we thought to get into the hot-ticket events. Kourtney comes trudging toward me, looking super sad. Even her giant hoop earrings seem to be drooping.

"What's up?" I take her arm. My program stalking can wait.

"I checked one more time in case there were places left in the beginners' vocal workshop," she says. She looks SO disappointed. "But it really is full. Oh well. Wasn't meant to be, I guess. I think there's a costume-display exhibition thing I can check out."

"Kourt! You know that's not the only vocal workshop on now," I chide. "Look—right here on the schedule, as discussed! Advanced vocal workshop. And the room is over there. The Sharpay Evans Ballroom."

I swivel her around and point at an open door. There's no Full sign in sight. Kourtney goes rigid, like a dog that doesn't want to be given a bath.

"Advanced, Nini! I'm not *advanced*. I'm a church singer, not a ballroom singer. You should have heard the other singers in the line."

"I heard them. They're not a patch on you."

"I don't want to sing in front of a whole ballroom of people," she argues.

"The workshop isn't taking up the whole ballroom. They put in fake walls to make the room smaller. Look."

I lead her (pull her) to the door. The room is big but it's not huge. Like I thought, the rest of the ballroom is closed off with folding doors. There are about thirty or forty seats, mostly filled, but there are still some empty places. No one else from our school is there. A man and a woman seem to be in charge, and they're handing out song sheets.

"Get in there," I whisper.

"What if I tank?" she whispers back.

"You don't know these people. It doesn't matter."

"Ladies?" the male teacher says. "Are you joining us?"

"My friend hasn't registered for this workshop, but do you still have places?" I ask, ignoring the fact that

Kourtney is smacking my back. "She's an excellent singer."

"Then come on in," the teacher says, and I practically shove Kourtney into the room. Before she has time to protest, I close the door and spin away.

Straight into Ricky.

"I thought you were doing a workshop with Kourtney now?" he says, peering at the closed door with suspicion.

"Change of plans!" I tell him, trying to sound breezy. I don't feel breezy. I feel stressed. I can't tell him that I need to spend my morning stalking famous people. Some of the stars are only going to stop by for an hour or two, so this is my big chance to grab them. I mean, we're not going to bump into them at the food court over lunch, are we?

"So you're free for the duets workshop later?" He looks all hopeful.

"Sure! Can't wait." What I mean is: I can't think about anything other than my mission. "Have a great morning! Gotta find Miss Jenn about . . . something. Then go to the restroom, and—yeah. I'll see you there!"

So I'm a liar and a secret keeper and a terrible girlfriend. But I want to be a *good* girlfriend. Right now that means being sneaky and being a stalker. Wait a second: Isn't this how E.J. was acting earlier this semester, when he thought he was being a good boyfriend by sneaking around behind my back, listening to messages on my phone, and . . . ?

No, Nini. This is completely different. This is sneakiness for a good cause.

Isn't it?

CHAPTER THIRTY-ONE

Freaking Out:
Workshop Edition

GINA

The songwriting workshop Ashlyn really wants to attend is later this morning, and she's only managed to squeeze onto the waitlist. This is SO disappointing for her, but I'm still hopeful they'll move it to a bigger room. Until then, we have time to fill. I trail around with her, suggesting possibilities.

Some girls we met in line bounce past, overexcited, both dressed in their cheerleading costumes. They've heard that Bayli Baker is here somewhere. They told us they've watched the YouTube video she made for Kenny Ortega about a thousand times, and they spent most of the wait in line braiding their hair like hers.

"Want to join them?" I ask Ashlyn, and she shakes her head.

"Let's find something we both want to do," she says, smiling at me. So maybe she's not mad. I hope not.

We're standing outside the Martha Cox Studio, and there's no Full sign on the door. The class is called "Music and Movement." Vague, but okay.

"How about this?" I suggest.

"It sounds like a dance workshop," Ashlyn says, sounding doubtful. "That's more your thing."

"It's not a *real* dance workshop," I tell her. "Look at the description. 'Movement and music: Want to own that cafeteria scene without sliding in hot cheese? Learn how to let go and get loose—but always hit your mark.'"

"Hmmm," says Ashlyn. "What was it you said E.J. was telling you? Something about letting go?"

"I know, right? Shall we give it a try?"

Before she has the chance to say no—not to mention Stick to the Status Quo—I grab her hand and draw her into the studio. This is a hotel ballroom, not a dance studio, so there aren't any barres or mirrors, and the floor is carpet tiles rather than boards.

"Let us begin," intones the teacher, who is slender, pale, and dressed all in black. "Everyone stand in a circle. The sacred circle of dance."

Ashlyn looks at me as if to say, *What the . . . ?*

"I know you may be here thinking you'll be leaping off cafeteria tables and dancing up and down stairs. That is the dream. But first you must be in touch with your own bodies."

"This sounds weird," whispers Ashlyn, and I have to agree.

"This is a new musical theater dance technique," the teacher continues, "that I have personally developed. It is revolutionizing school productions across this great nation through its superior pedagogical system. You must leave your preconceptions at the door. Also your shoes."

Ashlyn and I exchange glances again. She's still looking super dubious. We take off our shoes in silence and rejoin the "sacred circle."

"Everyone shake your hands. Let your heads go limp and flop around. Now I want to hear flopping noises. Everyone!"

"Flop," I say. I don't know how to make a flopping noise.

"Flop," says Ashlyn. Nobody else seems to know what to do.

"Flop-op-op-op-pop-pop-pop," says the teacher, shaking herself like a rag doll and collapsing onto the floor, still making the *flop-op-op* sounds. We all copy her.

I feel like a fish that's been caught and thrown into a bucket, flopping around, wishing I was back in the water.

Or maybe I'm Gabriella's cheesy fries, sailing through the air and about to smack, with a big sticky slurp, onto Sharpay's mock-Chanel jacket.

"Flop-op-op!" shrieks the teacher.

I think this workshop may have been a mistake.

CHAPTER THIRTY-TWO

Freaking Out: Workshop Edition

KOURTNEY

OMG. Why did I let Nini talk me into this? Or, specifically, push me into this ballroom of fear? I feel less "advanced" with every passing second.

We start with two super-intimidating things. First the teachers introduce themselves, and it turns out they are famous voice coaches who everyone else in the room has heard of and is in awe of, etc. They've worked on Broadway, they've worked in Hollywood. They've coached singers for films and national tours. What am I doing in this workshop??? I'll open my mouth and they'll know right away I'm not advanced at all. I should be retreating. To the beginners' class, to sit outside and listen through the wall.

The second intimidating thing is everyone else. We start with vocal warm-ups, like scales and Sharpay-and-Ryan-style mouth movements. I can already hear that some of the people in this room (maybe all) have experience. One of them sounds like an opera singer, even though she's my age. They can all project like I've never heard in my life. You'd think they were carrying around personal microphones.

I may look confident, but I don't know anything about technique or musical theory. Nini knows words like *legato* and *portamento*, but I generally know English words. When the teachers are talking, I realize I have no idea of the difference between head and chest registers. I've heard Miss Jenn talk about staggered breathing when people sing as a group, so everyone doesn't gasp for air at the same time. But I'm still not sure exactly where my diaphragm is. Or what it is. Or what I'm supposed to be doing with it.

Then the worst thing of all happens. Someone is picked to stand up at the front and sing a few lines of a song of their choice to everyone. In front of everyone. Out loud. I had thought—hoped—that we'd spend this session singing as a group. Not do the public-shaming thing.

Even worse than the worst thing of all: The girl who stands up sounds really, really good. She's no older than sixteen, I'd say, but she could be the voice of Moana. I am wowed and utterly intimidated at the same time. But the teachers actually criticize her for "scooping." Everyone else seems to know what that is, and they all frown and write things in their notebooks. I must be looking confused, because one of the teachers glances at me and decides to explain.

"Scooping," she says, "is when you slide up to the right pitch rather than beginning on the note itself. Sometimes it's fine, and works with the particular song, but it can seem lazy if you overuse it. It sounds as though you can't hit the note cleanly."

I nod and lower my head, thinking, *Please don't pick me next please don't pick me next please don't pick me ever.*

I think this workshop may have been a mistake.

CHAPTER THIRTY-THREE

Freaking Out:
Workshop Edition

RICKY

Nini has disappeared somewhere. Big Red isn't here yet. E.J. is on his way to collect him. I see Ashlyn and Gina go into a dance workshop, but the description on the door sounds weird. Miss Jenn and Carlos are hurling themselves at some boring-sounding panel. I'm not really interested in show business, as such, though Carlos was singing a song about it in the shower this morning. (There's no business like it, apparently. I'll take his word for it.)

Natalie walks by, and I shout to get her attention.

"Where are you headed?" I ask her.

"It's called 'Bet On It: Beginners' Choreography.' Want to come?"

"I guess." It's got the word *beginner* in it, so it can't be too bad.

We find the Country Club ballroom, which is huge. There are maybe a hundred of us in here and there's still plenty of space. The room looks strange and it takes me a moment to realize why. There's a bright green carpet on the floor, the color of Astroturf or whatever E.J. was drinking this morning.

"Cool!" Natalie says. "Just like the golf course."

"Which?"

Natalie rolls her eyes. "In *HSM2*, duh! When Troy sings 'Bet On It.' My favorite part is where he looks at his own reflection in the lake. What's yours?"

"I guess where he's running and jumping," I say. I'm starting to worry about what we're expected to do in this workshop.

"Okay, my Trojan soldiers!" shouts a young guy at the front. He seems to be the teacher, though he doesn't look much older than us. He's wearing dark pants and a polo shirt, like Troy in the movie, and his hair is combed forward and flicked.

"A total Troy wannabe," Natalie mutters to me.

"So today, if you haven't guessed, we're going to re-choreograph the 'Bet On It' number from *HSM2*. Each of you will play the part of Troy. We'll power out the song

185

and then we'll be improvising. Nothing is right or wrong here! Just feel the music and act it out. And try not to bump into each other!"

"Shall we try another workshop?" I mutter to Natalie. She checks the schedule.

"There's a craft workshop we could do, on how to bring *HSM* into your daily life and home decor. Actually, it sounds pretty cool. Macramé, crocheting, candles, mood boards—"

"Let's stay in this one," I say quickly. The approach to Beginners' Choreography may seem pretty random, but I'm more of a jumping-around guy than a whatever-macramé-is guy.

Everyone else is moving to the far reaches of the room, clearing some space, swinging their arms. If we all start leaping and jumping and gesturing like Troy, there's no way we can avoid hitting each other. In the actual movie, there was an actual golf course, and actual hills, and actual rocks, and an actual lake. Here we have a few feet each of lurid green carpet.

"I'll walk around to see who's doing what!" shouts Faux Troy. "I'll pick the best movers to showcase their moves for everyone else after the track ends!"

"I thought this was for beginners," Natalie says,

instantly worried. "I don't think I can take this level of pressure. You know, it's not too late to crochet."

"You can't be worse than me," I say, doing some crazy running-on-the-spot to distract her. Faux Troy spots me and points in our direction.

"Great move, curly dude!" he bellows, and everyone turns to look at me. "Save it for the dance! But I will be calling you up for the showcase!"

"Great," I say through gritted teeth.

"Better you than me," says Natalie, looking relieved. "Break out that move again? I can film you for Insta."

I think this workshop may have been a mistake.

CHAPTER THIRTY-FOUR

Freaking Out:
Workshop Edition

CARLOS

Miss Jenn and I run to the production panel. Literally run. It's not easy: Miss Jenn is in heels, and my patent leather shoes skid on this cheap carpet. Also, there are about a thousand people in our way.

"We have to get in," Miss Jenn mutters to me. "We *have* to. I don't care how many people we have to trample. This is it for us, Carlos. I'm deadly serious."

I know she is. The production panel includes people from the movie production team and from theater as well, talking about staging productions of *High School Musical 2*. You know, it wouldn't be my own personal pick for our spring show. I've seen the first movie—the *real* movie—thirty-seven times, but only the first fifteen minutes of each sequel. That was enough. I mean, *HSM2* doesn't even take place at East High, apart from the first number. But Miss Jenn seems to have her heart set on it, and Miss Jenn is my leader, mentor, and unicorn.

She's also kind of panicked today, as though she's competing in a roller derby. After a lot of strategic elbowing, we manage to get somewhere near the door. Just in time to see it close and the Full sign go up.

"No!" Miss Jenn shrieks.

"I guess we're not the only school planning that show," I tell her. I feel really bad for Miss Jenn. A lot of things haven't gone as the way we hoped they would this past semester—i.e., almost getting fired, burning down the theater, and so on. "Maybe you could tell them who you are, and pull some strings to get in."

Miss Jenn turns to me, looking a whole lot less than her usual perky self.

"Carlos," she says, her voice low and serious. "Nobody knows me. Nobody remembers me. I was one of many in the background of the movie, and if I have any fame at all from it, it's because my one line got cut. I don't think Kenny Ortega could pick me out of a police lineup, even if I was dressed as a Wildcats cheerleader and holding an apple."

"That can't be true," I say. I've never seen her so low.

I've never seen her give in. She always sees the bright side of things, and somehow makes magic happen.

"Let's face it," she says, leaning against a wall. From inside the room we can hear applause and laughing. "So far our research trip is kind of a disaster. We arrived late and missed everything on Friday night. We missed early registration. Now we're missing the main panel I wanted to attend. I was planning to ask a question, get hold of the mic, introduce myself. . . ."

"We could go to a meet-and-greet," I suggest, trying to make the best of things.

"Look at these crowds! We can't get close to any cast members. Every single person here is wearing *HSM* merchandise or costumes, so we can't stand out. Even our school van can't stand out because everyone else here is pretending they go to 'East High' as well. I can't make us special and different. I can't get us noticed. If we want our next musical to be game-changing, we need a guest star."

"It's still early in the day," I tell her, though it's hard not to feel downhearted. "E.J. would say we have to go with the flow."

"And Stick to the Status Quo?" she asks. *Touché.*

I hate seeing Miss Jenn like this. She's convinced herself that to make something big out of our school, we need star power, an injection of *HSM* magic. She wants everything bigger and better next semester, and I get that. We want a big stage and a big audience. She wants to put our school on the map—our real school, I mean, and a real map. It's not enough to be an *HSM* tourist attraction. She wants to be a place that nurtures performers and produces its own stars.

"I think everything I've done may have been a mistake," she tells me, and I squeeze her hand. This is not the time to sing "There's No Business Like Show Business."

So I hum it instead, under my breath, and hope that a little of its magic will rub off on Miss Jenn. I want her to be happy again. I want us all to be happy. Whatever show we do next semester, we'll make it a success—guest star or not.

CHAPTER THIRTY-FIVE

KOURTNEY

The time has come. It's my turn to sing in front of everyone.

It's near the end of the workshop, and I was hoping that we'd run out of time. I am super nervous. This feeling is unfamiliar to me, and I've been trying my best to overcome it. I sit there thinking, *What would Harriet Tubman do? What would Ada Lovelace do? What would Susan B. Anthony do?*

But most important right now: *What would Kourtney do?* And the answers are a) sing in a loud and incoherent series of squeaks, while everyone laughs; b) crumple into a heap on the floor and have to be carried out; or c) all of the above.

No one has done too badly yet, though some of the

other kids are clearly nervous as well. There are some good singers in the room. Really good singers. The girl sitting next to me, Carlota, is carrying a YAC bag; she's been at the conservatory in Denver for three semesters, she said. I wish I could tell her about Nini starting in the new year, but I'm sworn to secrecy.

When it was Carlota's turn to sing, she was amazing. She sounded like a Broadway star, every word crystal clear and she had that wobbly effect—the teachers called it *vibrato*—at the end of lines. She was acting while she sang, and making gestures, as though she was onstage and this was a real audience in a theater. I can't do any of that. All I can do is sing.

"Kourtney, is it?" Diane, the female teacher, is waving me up. "What are you going to sing for us?"

I shuffle out of my seat and make my way up to the front, face burning. I may have left my makeup bag in the van, but I don't need extra blush today. Carlota sang something really complicated, up and down, with really fast words. I'd been planning to sing something from *High School Musical*, but the teachers said we shouldn't. My mind is blank. What should I sing?

"Kourtney?" Diane asks again, with the briefest of smiles. "Song?"

"'Amazing Grace,'" I tell her. It's the first thing that

pops into my head. Not very original, or very complicated. I mean, someone earlier sang an actual opera aria!

"Great." Diane nods. "When you're ready."

I take a deep breath and look out at the room. The other kids in the room are strangers to me, but they're smiling in a supportive way, I think. They don't seem mean or competitive. They don't seem to be waiting for me to fail.

"Go, Kourtney!" Carlota calls and everyone laughs. Some of my tension dissolves.

I open my mouth, trying to summon up the first note. We sing this at church all the time. It was my grandmother's favorite hymn. When she sang it, it sounded rich and deep, straight from the heart. I don't know another way to sing it.

The first line. The second line. I manage to get them out, without any embellishment, without falling over. Then I stop. I don't think the teachers will want to hear any more. Not of a church girl singing a church song.

"Go on," says Diane. "Do you know the second verse?"

I nod. It's all I can do to sing, let alone speak. So I pretend I'm back in church, the way I did when Miss Jenn asked me to sing during tech rehearsal that one time. I imagine the light pouring in the high windows and the smiling faces of the congregation. I've been singing in church since I was a kid, and it's always been a happy place for me.

Thinking of this makes me so much more relaxed. I pour everything into that old hymn, that simple melody. It's so pure and true. In a song like "Amazing Grace," you can lose yourself in the words and the tune. I hear my voice ringing out in the room, as though it's coming from another person, another place.

When I stop singing, everyone claps—real applause, Carlota whooping, and big smiles everywhere I look. I really did it. I sang in front of a room of strangers. Nobody booed. Nobody sneered. I didn't collapse.

"Thanks, Kourtney. Good." Diane is smiling. She faces the rest of the singers. "Do you see how strong a line can sound without embellishment? Kourtney's pitch is good, so that helps."

"She's almost a little sharp," says Dan, the other teacher. "Pavarotti was like that. It meant his voice could reach just above the note, and hit it true. So there's none of that swooping up that we discussed earlier."

"And she's not singing from the chest," Diane tells them. Everyone is taking notes. What? "So it doesn't sound strained."

"Or nasal," Dan points out. "Though if you relaxed your shoulders more, Kourtney, you'd open up the sound."

"Which doesn't mean making it louder," Diane says to the class. "It means controlling it more, and allowing it to flow."

They say other things but my ears are ringing. All the criticism is constructive. They're treating me as though I'm like the others, a real singer. I can't believe it.

I'm the last person to be workshopped. We gather up our things, and I say goodbye to Carlota. She gives me a hug, and that's when I realize I'm still shaking.

On the way out of the room, Diane stops me.

"Thanks for coming along today, Kourtney," she says. "What experience do you have as a singer?"

I tell her about my church, and I tell her where I go to school. That I plan to audition for the spring musical.

"Your first time auditioning for a school production?" She sounds surprised.

"Usually I do makeup and wardrobe," I say. Diane shakes her head.

"Well, say goodbye to backstage," she says. "You have a lot of raw talent. It needs nurturing so you don't ruin your voice belting everything out. But do you see how natural and unforced you sound compared with some of the others today? Many young singers are too mannered and theatrical. So work on your breathing and tone, but never lose your own sound. It's really fresh and special."

I leave the workshop buzzing. BUZZING. Where is Nini? I need to find her and tell her everything. She was right. I'm so glad she made me come to this workshop.

The hallways are crowded with people changing sessions and everything's a blur again. Maybe I need to find somewhere quiet to sit down. I think about what E.J. said this morning, when he was being all chill and super happy. He said we should live in the moment more and not stress about what other people think. I was so worried about how people would react, so sure I would fail. All that anxiety for nothing!

Maybe in this workshop today I was touched by a little of my grandmother's own amazing grace. I close my eyes and think of her face, smiling at me. She always says that there's nothing she loves more than listening to me sing.

CHAPTER THIRTY-SIX

ASHLYN

Our workshop runs late. We're supposed to have finished, and I can hear the noise outside of everyone coming out of sessions and making their way to new ones. But Gina and I are still trapped in this room. We've dubbed it the Dungeon of Strange Movements. All this time we've been making shapes with our bodies and whirling like dervishes. It wasn't exactly dancing and it wasn't exactly drama. But it was a lot of fun.

When the teacher finally says we can stop, we collapse on the floor, laughing.

"That was weird," Gina says, lying back with her legs in the air. "I've done more strenuous workouts, but there's something exhausting about being strange."

"Flop-op-op," I say, and we both start laughing again.

"Hey," Gina says, sitting up and feeling for her discarded shoes. "I'm really sorry about before."

"What happened before?" I'm puzzled.

"The bad advice I gave you last night," she says, "about texting Big Red. I shouldn't have pretended to be someone I'm not. Old habits, I guess."

"Don't worry about it," I tell her. "Really, it's forgotten. And luckily, Big Red is not here right now, so I don't have to think about him anymore."

"I just want you and me to be friends," says Gina, and she looks so vulnerable all of a sudden—not tough Gina anymore, not haughty or aloof. Just a girl who's spent too much time alone, and too much time on the move.

"Well, we have something in common," I say. "Music."

"You're the musician! I'm a performer, but not a composer like you. It's such a shame that the composing workshop is full."

"I know." I'm trying not to be too bummed about it. "But lots of people never get opportunities like this—you know, a convention, or a workshop. They keep on writing songs at home or at school, or while they're waiting for a bus. They don't let anything get in the way of their dreams."

"Not even flopping noises?" Gina asks, and we laugh so loudly that the teacher, packing up her strange black bag, gives us a long look.

We get our shoes on and join the fray outside. There's a seminar down the hall discussing story arcs in the *HSM* movies, and we decide to go to that.

"It's pretty nerdy, I know," I say to Gina when we join the line to get in. "But we're all nerds here. That's what makes us secretly cool."

"I never wanted to be a nerd," Gina tells me, leaning against the wall. "I guess I was just in denial. I didn't want other people to judge me."

"Who cares what other people think?" I say. "Look at us. We've just been flopping like fish and hopping like toads. And why?"

"Absolutely no idea."

I really hope Gina's mom lets her stay with my family next semester. Not just because Gina can stay at our school rather than move again. It's a chance for us to get to know each other more, to be nerds together, and to become even better friends.

Insta Interlude

Following

E.J. here, and not where you'd expect me to be. That's how I roll these days—confounding expectations. By these days I mean today, really. Is it still today? I feel as though I've been up for hours.

Anyway, I'm at a gas station in Idaho, waiting for Big Red to arrive. I skipped the morning sessions to come collect him. The sky is blue. The snow has gone. I seem to have green juice all over my clothes, but it's not the end of the world. It's organic, at least.

Hopefully we'll get to the convention in time for afternoon workshops and some *HSM* fun. We're not planning to stay for the final session, because it's just a sing-along.

Hey! I spot the Big-Red-mobile pulling in! Time to drive back to Wyoming and Wildcat it up. Also to try to get this green stuff off my clothes.

E.J. out.

1200 likes

Add a comment...

CHAPTER THIRTY-SEVEN

BIG RED

E.J. drops me off at the hotel entrance so I can register and then meet up with everyone else at the food hall for lunch. I'm so psyched to be here, even if I've missed most of the morning activities. There's time this afternoon for a couple of workshops, and maybe I can spot some stars. Hang out with Ricky as well, of course, and cheer him up.

And avoid Ashlyn. It's all too complicated—girls, life, relationships, whatever. Luckily, there are about a thousand people here, most of them dressed like cheerleaders, and it's easy to get lost in the crowd.

Until I turn a corner and bump straight into Ashlyn and Gina.

"Hey!" I say, and Ashlyn says nothing. She looks so startled, I guess Ricky didn't tell her I was coming.

"Your favorite word," says Gina, eyebrows raised. I don't get it.

"Oh . . . you're here," Ashlyn says. I guess Ricky did tell her I was coming, but she doesn't seem that excited about it. "I mean, weren't you working?"

People are barging past us, so we all shuffle toward a wall. I'm glad for something to lean against.

"My cousin could work for me after all," I explained. "As it turns out."

I don't know why I added that bit. I never say things like *as it turns out*. That's something my dad would say. I think I may be spending too much time with old people.

"How did you get here?" Gina asks.

"My mom drove me half the way, then E.J. picked me up."

"E.J.?" Both of the girls shout his name in unison.

"But we saw him here this morning, when we were in line," Ashlyn says to Gina, as though I'm not here.

"He offered to collect me someplace in Idaho."

"What happened to him at that meditation convention?" Gina asks Ashlyn. Again, as though I'm not here. I heard all about the "other" convention in the car ride here. E.J. had a great time, as well as various epiphanies, he said. I didn't tell him that I don't know what *epiphany* means.

I want to ask Ashlyn why she didn't reply to my last

text, but it would sound needy and pathetic, and maybe I don't want to hear the answer. She looks embarrassed right now, and probably I do, too.

"You guys!" Kourtney arrives to save the embarrassing day. "Has anyone seen Miss Jenn? I want to get the keys to the van. Nini and I left our costumes in there."

"I'll go!" I shout. "I'll go find her. And get your stuff."

Kourtney describes her bag to me, while Gina and Ashlyn mutter away. Maybe I should have stayed in Salt Lake. Maybe I should stay hiding in the van. I really need to get away from this situation with Ashlyn.

On my way to find Miss-Jenn-in-the-haystack, I manage to bump into someone I really want to see: Ricky. At least he's pleased to see me. Briefly.

"Have you seen Nini anywhere?" he asks me, frowning. "She's been acting kind of odd, and I'm starting to feel like she's avoiding me. She's not answering my texts. I have no idea what's going on."

Maybe all girls are angry today. I don't understand them at all.

We walk to the food hall, looking for Miss Jenn. Ricky says once we get the keys, he'll come to the van with me to help carry the stuff. . . .

We find Miss Jenn deep in conversation with Carlos, and get the keys from her. Her directions for the school van are vague—we're basically looking for a van that's parked in a snow drift somewhere between here and the city limits, from what I can tell. But Ricky and I retrieve our winter gear from coat check before we start our trek into the unknown.

"Girls are hard to figure out," I say to Ricky, and he nods.

"You're telling me," he says, checking his phone one more time.

CHAPTER THIRTY-EIGHT

NINI

So every single one of the meet-and-greets is over, and my tally of autographs? Zero. How could I be so completely useless at this? I missed every single workshop, panel, and seminar this morning in order to get the signatures for Ricky, and I don't have a single one yet. I couldn't even get anywhere near Sharpay's Yorkie puppy. At one point I thought a guy dressed as a skater dude was an actual skater dude from the movie, but he turned out to be a teacher from a school in New Mexico. Weird, and slightly disturbing.

I tried: I really did. Maybe stalking isn't my strong point. When I spotted Ms. Darbus, aka Alyson Reed, I followed her along five hallways to the women's bathroom before I lost her. Maybe I should have crawled along the ground, looking under the door of each stall to try to locate her, but that seemed a little too much. I might have gotten her signature, but I might also have been escorted off the premises by security.

By the time I squeezed my way into Monique Coleman's meet-and-greet, she was waving goodbye from the signing table and being ushered out a no-public-access side door. The closest I got to Ashley was the back of a cheering crowd chanting "We want 'Fabulous!'" I'm not even sure if Ashley herself was there, or if everyone was just having a Sharpay moment. Another fail.

I feel pretty defeated. It's almost time to meet everyone else at the food court for lunch, so I spin on my heel—and bump into someone. The kind of crash that sends both people reeling.

"I'm so sorry!" I say, because I know this was totally my fault, scrambling to pick up my program. Not that anyone would want to steal it; there's not a single autograph on it. Whoever I bumped into picks it up and hands it to me.

"Don't lose this!" says a guy's voice. I recognize that voice. I recognize that face. I can't believe it, but it's Lucas Grabeel! In person. The real thing. If only Miss Jenn were here! She would probably faint.

"You . . . I—I mean, could you?"

"You want me to sign this?" he asks, smiling, and I nod. I can't even find my pen, but luckily he has one. He signs the cover with a flourish. At last I have a signature, and not just that—I have *Lucas Grabeel's* signature.

"Were you at the rest stop on I-15 last night, where our van broke down?" I manage to ask him.

"That was you?" He smiles again and hands me back my program. "I'm glad you guys got here in the end."

"You know we're the real East High," I blurt out. "In Salt Lake City. Where you filmed—you know."

"That is so cool," he says. "I'm really glad we got the chance to meet. I'm just on my way out."

And just like that handlers appear at his elbows and steer him away. Other people are running after him, waving their programs, but it doesn't look as though he's stopping. I was so, so lucky. I almost don't mind missing out on some other signatures. Hopefully Ricky won't mind either.

If I grab lunch quickly, I can get in the line for Ashley Tisdale (I see a sign, and it turns out she *is* here!). Then I'll have the most amazing gift for Ricky, the ultimate souvenir. And maybe he'll understand why I have to miss the duets workshop I promised we'd do together. This signed program will make it up to him. I hope.

CHAPTER THIRTY-NINE

#MissJennSadface

1. Lunchtime. Really? You feel as though you've been here for twelve hours already. Twelve useless hours of achieving very little. The kids assemble in the food court, where they make poor nutritional choices, but at least most of them seem happy and excited. Natalie is buzzing; her puppy necklace was a hit with the owner of Sharpay's Yorkie puppy. You're glad someone is getting something out of this debacle.

2. Carlos looks forlorn. He's the one you've really let down. You made big promises and plans, and none of them are working out. You need a

lift. Carlos needs a lift. There are no lifts visible in the food hall.

3. Hear Nini announce that she not only met but *talked* to Lucas Grabeel. OMG! He *was* the guy at the rest stop last night. Nini even got his autograph, though she swears you to secrecy and says under no circumstances can you reveal this to Ricky. (Drama!) Apparently she told LG that her school was the real East High where he spent time filming. A beacon of light shines! Not literally, because there are no windows in the food court and all the lights here are fluorescent. But still.

4. Race off to see if you can find LG. He's here somewhere. He knows about your school. He saw your van getting fixed in the snow last night. He waved and smiled at you all (and mainly at you). He's talked to Nini and signed her program. (Which you must not mention to Ricky, etc.) But at the registration desk they tell you he's just left. Sorry. He has a family thing to get to in another state. He'd already stayed much longer than planned.

5. Return to the food hall feeling defeated. See everyone's faces. They all look low when they should be happy. Oh boy. Today is turning into nothing but lost opportunities. How can you make dreams come true for these kids when you're failing at every single dream of your own?

CHAPTER FORTY

RICKY

By the time I turned up to lunch with Big Red, Nini had come and gone. Miss Jenn said something vague about things Nini needed to wrap up. Kourtney took the costumes we'd uncovered—after a *long* walk to find the van—and *also* said something vague about things Nini needed to wrap up. Sigh. If she's going outside, she'll need to wrap up warm. But I have no idea where she is. This convention is chaos.

I tell Big Red that Nini is meeting me at the duets workshop, so he heads off in another direction. Pretty much runs off, actually, because there's something awkward going on with him and Ashlyn that I can't even pretend to understand.

When the duets workshop is about to begin, Nini still

isn't here. I prop my guitar up by the door (I rescued it from the van at lunchtime) and stand near it so Nini can find me easily. But the teacher closes the door because we're about to begin, and still no Nini.

I can't believe she's missing this. Why has she been so strange today—and so frantic? It's like she's on some kind of mission. Whenever I see her, she's so sweet, so I know she's not trying to avoid me. Not really. But this convention has made her act crazy. Maybe it's making us all act kind of crazy. There are so many people here, and about 90 percent of them are dressed as cheerleaders.

The only person I recognize in the room is E.J., and he makes a beeline for me. His cheeks look red from where he must have been rubbing at that green stuff earlier.

"Hey, thanks again for driving Big Red here," I tell him.

"Where is he?" E.J. asks.

"At a production workshop with Natalie, I think. More his style than singing, he said."

"So, want to partner up?" E.J. asks. "Everyone else is in a pair already."

"Nini is supposed to be coming," I tell him.

"Last time I saw her she was heading toward the final meet-and-greet. I think she's hoping to see Ashley Tisdale."

"Really?" I don't think E.J. is right, but there's no time to argue.

"Everyone stand with your duet partner," the teacher calls, closing the door. He's a big guy, with a deep speaking voice, wearing an argyle vest that matches his socks.

"Until Nini gets here," E.J. says, grinning at me, "let's go with the flow."

This new philosophical E.J. is almost as annoying as the old E.J.—and at least the old E.J. didn't give advice all the time. I know, I should be grateful to him for giving up his entire morning driving for hours to collect Big Red from Idaho. He's a pretty generous person. But that doesn't mean I want to sing duets with him.

"Take each other's hands," calls the teacher. Really? Okay. "Look straight into each other's eyes."

E.J. gazes at me as though we're in some kind of staring contest, or maybe he's trying to see deep into my soul. All I want to do is blink.

"People think duets are just about learning the words and music," the teacher tells us, "and trying not to drown each other out. But the real place to start with any duet is to locate your energy, which might be positive or negative. Who are you? Who is the other person? What do you want from them? What do you fear in them?"

E.J. squints at me, so I squint back. All I really want from him is to let my hands go.

"Find the tension between you and your partner," the teacher goes on. "There's always some tension in a duet. It may be romantic. It may be antagonistic. You two may be plotting something against another. You may be working against each other. A duet can be a conversation. It can be an argument. It can be two different positions, posited and revealed in the course of one song."

"Do we have to hold hands the whole time?" someone asks, and we all laugh with nervous relief.

"No questions!" snaps the teacher. "Now, we'll begin by speaking, not singing, the words from a song that was cut from *High School Musical*. It's one of the extra tracks you can get, and my personal favorite. It has a lot of personal meaning to me. After the break-up of my relationship—"

"Ah, TMI!" someone says, and we all squirm and try not to laugh.

"But none of us know the words," another person points out, and the teacher raises his voice.

"They're projected on the screen! Take a moment to read them, then make sure you're holding hands and looking into each other's eyes."

"But what if we forget the words, and we can't look at

the screen because we're looking into each other's eyes?"

"I will feed you the lines!" he barks. "Here they are. The song is called 'Love Is True, Love Is Real.'"

"You know," E.J. says to me in a low voice, "I don't remember this song at all, and I've listened to all the extra tracks. He probably wrote it himself."

We stand reading the lyrics. They're pretty sappy, and there's no way I'll remember them.

"Turn to each other again," shouts the teacher. "One of you will take the Troy part, and the other will be Gabriella."

"I call Troy," says E.J., gripping my hands even tighter.

"And remember," the teacher booms, "maintain eye contact at all times. Look deeply into each other's eyes and say the words as though you mean them."

"'Love is the strangest kind of thing,'" E.J. begins.

"Hang on—I didn't agree to be Gabriella."

"I called Troy."

"Well, just because you called it doesn't mean I agree."

"Gentlemen!" the teacher calls. "Lyrics only, please."

"'Love is the strangest kind of thing,'" E.J. recites again. "'It arrives out of the blue.'"

I sigh, and glance at the screen. "'It may be here, then disappear, so what are we to do?'"

"'But we're in love, right here and now.'" How can

E.J. remember this stuff so easily? "'It's a very special time.'"

Another glance at the screen. Why do I have to be Gabriella?

"'A time to tell each other this,'" I mutter, "'and know the feeling's right.'"

"Take a step closer to each other," calls the teacher, "and let's have the first verse again. Louder voices this time. Remember, speak as though you really mean it."

"'Love is the strangest kind of thing,'" shouts E.J., his broccoli breath blasting my face. "'It arrives out of the blue.'"

"'It may be here,'" I shout back, "'then disappear, so what are we to do?!'"

E.J. squeezes my hands again. "'But we're in love, right here and now! It's a very special time!'"

"Um, 'A time to tell each other this and know the feeling's right.'"

"With more *actual* feeling, if you please," says the teacher, so close to my left ear I almost jump out of my skin. "How can you sing the words if you can't say them?"

E.J. smiles at me as though he feels sorry for me.

"Dude, we have to convey emotion through our eyes."

I know what emotions I'd like to convey right now.

"And again!" calls Mr. Argyle, and half the room

shouts, "'LOVE IS THE STRANGEST KIND OF THING, IT ARRIVES OUT OF THE BLUE.'"

Where is Nini???

I think this workshop may have been a mistake.

CHAPTER FORTY-ONE

NINI

I have to admit defeat. Almost two hours in the line waiting so Ashley Tisdale can sign my program, and before I'm even within sight of her, we're told she has to leave. Initially she was only supposed to be here this morning, so it was a big deal that she stayed as long as she did. It is so disappointing, but what can I do? I've tried my best. Hopefully Ricky will be happy with what I've done. I did manage to nab Lucas Grabeel, after all. That's a major score.

When the line closes, I make my way to the duet workshop, thinking that maybe I can catch the end of it. I promised Ricky I'd be there, and I know I've let him down. But once he sees his gift, he won't be able to be mad at me. I hope not, anyway.

Once again, I'm too late. People are pouring out of the room. Ricky plods out, head down, carrying his guitar. He does *not* look happy.

"Ricky!" I wave at him, smiling, but he doesn't smile back.

"Where have you been?" he says in a plaintive voice. He's hurt rather than angry, and it makes my stomach twist. If he's this sad when I'm not around for a workshop, how will he cope with me living in Denver for an entire semester?

"How was the workshop?" I ask. I want him to be in a happier mood before I give him the program.

"Weird. I had to partner with E.J.," he says. "It was a love duet."

I try not to laugh. "Where is he now?"

"Still in there," Ricky says. "I think he's giving relationship advice to the teacher. I have no idea what's going on with him today."

"The teacher or E.J.?"

"Both."

We walk down the crowded hallway, jostled by everyone racing to whatever they're doing next. I've been on my feet all day, mainly standing in lines, and it's a relief to spot some chairs by a big window, overlooking a snowy courtyard.

"Could we sit down for a while?" I ask Ricky. Now he looks worried.

"Is everything okay?" We pull some chairs together to the corner, away from a school group who are flopped out, eating snacks. I'm not the only person who's exhausted.

"Everything's fine. Really."

"It's just you're being so mysterious." Ricky props his guitar case against one of the chairs. "Why did you say you would meet me at the workshop if you didn't think you could come?"

"I thought I could get there in time," I tell him, though this isn't strictly true. Eek. I hate all these secrets. "But . . ."

"But what? What's really going on?"

I take a deep breath. I can reveal one secret now— just not the big secret, the mega secret, of where I might be going to school after the holidays. But at least I have something to show for all the sneaking around.

"This is for you," I say, and pull out the signed program. Ricky takes it, puzzled. "Look inside."

He starts turning pages and his face lights up. In a short time, I've managed to get seven different cast members and four crew from the original movie to sign different pages—some by their own photos, some next to behind-the-scenes shots from filming, and some around the big East Side High shot in the center of the program.

"Wow," says Ricky, smiling at last. Some of the messages are personalized—like, *To Ricky Bowen, the next Troy Bolton* or *Hey, Ricky, you're so fine, you're so fine you blow my mind, hey, Ricky!* (That last one is an '80s song reference, apparently. One of my moms will know.)

"Is this really Lucas Grabeel's signature?" he asks, eyes widening.

"You won't believe this, but I bumped into him," I say and tell him the whole story. Ricky can't believe that Lucas was the guy we saw at the rest stop last night.

"I thought it was one of Miss Jenn's dreams," he says. "This is amazing. But I don't get it. Why did you get this for *me*? I mean, why did you spend all this time and miss every workshop and panel to do this?"

I'm not sure what to say, or how to begin. "I just wanted to give you something really special" is the best I can manage. "*High School Musical* is . . . important to us. Right?"

"Sure." He grins. "It's the first musical I ever liked. I only auditioned so I could be close to you again."

"And your evil plan worked!" I joke. "So, it has meaning for us. I thought getting all the signatures on the program would be . . . I don't know. The best present ever."

"Nini." Ricky shakes his head. "Did you ever think that spending time together today at workshops would be the best present ever? You and me, having fun, singing songs? Holding hands?"

He rummages in the free *HSM* canvas bag we all got at registration until he finds a Wildcats pen. He holds it out to me.

"What?" I don't know what he wants me to do.

"Nini Salazar-Roberts, would you please sign my program?"

"But I'm not one of the original cast, silly." It's such a cute gesture, I have to admit.

"You're one of *my* original cast. And anyway, the only signature I ever really want on a program is *yours*. Although, sure, getting Lucas's signature is pretty cool."

"It better be." I pretend to hit him with the program. "This took me hours!"

He makes me sign the cover. "This way I can sell it when you're famous," he jokes, and I can't resist giving him a kiss.

Ricky tells me about a song he's been trying to write, called "Confusion," but he says he's getting nowhere with it.

"I've been meaning to write a song as well," I say, "for Kourtney. I realized in all this time she and I have been best friends, I've never written a song just for her. That's crazy, right? But everything has been so busy with school, and this, and rehearsing for the fundraising concert."

Ricky gets that *I've-had-a-brilliant-idea* look on his face.

"Let's try to find somewhere more quiet," he says. "I'd suggest the van, but it's miles away, and really cold. But maybe there's a corner somewhere here where we can sit down and work on the song together. Not my song, I mean. But yours."

"Really?" I ask. "You'll help me with a song for Kourtney?"

"Of course. There's always something special about your songs. And when we work together . . ."

"It's better. I know." We give each other big smiles, and for the first time today I don't feel so anxious. Ricky and I will get to spend time together, not at workshops or seminars or panels, or any of the things we thought we'd be doing here, but writing a song together. For someone else.

"All of E.J.'s talk about being selfless must be rubbing off on me," Ricky says with a grin. "Better than the green stuff he spilled all over his clothes."

He grabs his guitar and we head down the corridor, looking for another nook. For the first time today I feel happy and relaxed. My big romantic gesture didn't turn out quite how I imagined, but Ricky seemed pleased with it.

"It's already starting to get dark outside," he observes, nodding at the dusky view outside. "This convention has gone so fast."

Everything's going too fast, I want to tell him. Life's going by so quickly. I wish we could stop, just for a while, and enjoy what we have—right here, right now.

CHAPTER FORTY-TWO

Miss Jenn's Top Five Regrets at #HSMCon

1. Not making it into the industry panel, where you could have revealed your identity, asked killer questions, and received invitations to the greenroom afterward. (There has to be a greenroom, right?)

2. Not making it into the Staging a Sequel panel, where you could have done all of the above, plus got some tips for the spring musical.

3. Exchanging texts with Mr. Mazzara at a particularly low moment this afternoon. Him: All going to plan with your non-educational

"fun" event? You: Nothing going to plan just yet but education triumphing, as ever. Him: Secured your "guest star" for the unnecessary extra musical this school year? (Who told him that was your plan? Maybe you, in a brazen moment of hubris. Yes, definitely you.) You: Watch this space!!! Him: I'll take that as a no.

4. Not making it anywhere near Ashley Tisdale, Lucas Grabeel, Monique Coleman, Olesya Rulin, Alyson Reed, or anyone who appeared, made, or in any way contributed to *High School Musical*.

5. Dragging Carlos into your hopeless quest for a guest star, which means dragging him into your hopeless quest for a bigger, better, shinier Act II to your life. That boy deserved to have some fun today, rather than run the corridors of despair with you. Admit it: He's Dorothy, not you. You're the Cowardly Lion. You need to think less about your own dreams, and work on making his come true.

CHAPTER FORTY-THREE

CARLOS

At five we all assemble in the hotel lobby. News flash: None of us have had the Best. Time. Ever. Maybe our expectations were too high. Maybe we were unrealistic. Shocker! We're drama kids. Our imaginations are out of control.

So here are the deets on the lobby scene. I work the room and get the lowdown, so I know how much I need to hide from Miss Jenn. (She is super-sad face right now, and keeps apologizing to me.)

Nini seems to have spent all her time at meet-and-greets, so has missed every single workshop, seminar, panel, and master class. What I will tell Miss Jenn: Nini scored a huge number of original-cast-and-crew signatures for her program, which she has given—INEXPLICABLY—to Ricky Bowen.

Pause to regain composure and stop my head exploding.

Speaking of Ricky, I hear he's spent his time jumping around on a fake golf course with Natalie and holding hands with E.J. while shouting love lyrics. What I will tell Miss Jenn: Ricky has new skills in choreography and duet performance. Also, he is the proud owner of the Best Souvenir Ever.

Pause again to regain composure and suppress ocean waves of jealous rage.

Big Red only arrived this afternoon, and spent most of his time looking for our van in the lot. E.J. has spent his weekend driving back and forth to Idaho and/or attending the wrong convention. Ashlyn couldn't get into the songwriters' workshop, so she and Gina have spent a lot of time flopping around like fish. Kourtney infiltrated an advanced vocal workshop and has been struck dumb with overawed-ness ever since.

As for me, I've been so preoccupied with hunting down possibles for Miss Jenn's guest-star slot, I didn't go to any of the choreography classes. All I've learned to do today is how to run down hallways dodging kids dressed as basketball players and cheerleaders and how to claw my way into industry sessions. I couldn't even get near Sharpay's Yorkie puppy.

I don't know. I really don't know. It's not like me to be lost for words, but I'm at a loss to spin this. When we look at the hard facts, we've missed most of the things we wanted to attend. Everyone is putting on a brave face, because the show must go on, even if our sole audience is Miss Jenn.

But there's the distinct aroma of disappointment in the air. We all look disheveled and deflated. Kourtney is carrying around a bag with costumes she and Nini never got a chance to wear. Gina has zipped up her top and pulled the hood over her hair, like a turtle retreating into its shell. If they had the energy to break into song right now, it would be "Stick to the Status Quo."

"Okay, people," Miss Jenn says in the brightest voice she can manage. This woman is my idol. She never admits defeat. "Why don't you all wait here, and I'll go and get the van? You all look tired. It's been a long day."

She pulls on a woolen hat and mittens. Her coat is red, and I can't help thinking she's Little Red Riding Hood, setting out on a long journey into the forest. (Well, the van *is* parked miles away.) Except Ms. Hood was looking forward to visiting her grandmother. She had no idea the wolf would be waiting. Today Miss Jenn has gone ten rounds with the wolf already, and is nursing some wounds.

"Hang on a second, Miss Jenn." E.J. steps forward. How can that boy still be flecked with green? "I have an announcement."

It better not be that he's met Ashley Tisdale, or I really will explode.

"What is it, E.J.?" Miss Jenn sounds fatigued, but she's trying her best to smile. "Everyone, gather round."

"Today, in the duets workshop I did with Ricky," E.J. says, beaming at us all, "I realized something."

"That you really need to wash your shirt?" asks Big Red. Everyone's so wiped out, this barely raises a laugh. E.J. isn't fazed at all. Though that boy is never fazed. He sails through life like a battleship—or maybe a luxury yacht.

"I realized," he says, "that while this convention is great and crazy and kind of overwhelming, that all of us, from East High, singing together—well, that's the most important thing. Today isn't about being a single star, but being a constellation together."

"Very nice sentiment," Miss Jenn says, smiling at him, the van keys jingling in her hand. "Thank you for saying that, E.J."

"So that's why we had to gather around?" Gina asks. "So E.J. could tell us we're a constellation?"

"What I'm saying is," E.J. continues, undeterred, "I think we should stay. For the sing-along?"

"What?" Everyone looks at him as though he's crazy. What was in that green concoction he drank this morning?

"We all love singing together," he tells us. "That's what makes us happy. That's what brings us together. And we all love *High School Musical*, otherwise we wouldn't be here. Why not celebrate what we love?"

Now I'm not the only one lost for words. It's not often you'll hear me utter this, but E.J. may be right. We were all so sure we didn't want to stay for the sing-along. But most of us have been here all day without getting the chance to sing at all. That is just wrong. The whole *HSM* spirit is to dance and sing as a group—in the cafeteria, on the basketball court, onstage.

Miss Jenn's eyes are shining.

"Well said," she tells E.J., dropping the keys into her bag. "What do the rest of you think? Should we stay or should we go?"

"We'll have to let our families know we're arriving home super late," Natalie points out. "They're expecting us to be leaving now."

"Will anyone's parents and/or guardians object?" Miss Jenn asks, and everyone assures her there'll be no problem.

Kourtney holds her bag up in the air. "I got makeup!"

"So we're agreed," E.J. says. "We're staying for the sing-along. Right?"

Just like that, the mood changes. Lights, camera, action. Everyone's buzzing. (I'd say everyone is feeling "All for One" right now, but you know I never make references to the sequels.) There's so much excited chatter, it feels like backstage on opening night. Everyone is texting home to say we'll be rolling in late.

"Love this energy," Miss Jenn whispers to me.

"I know," I say, pleased that she's happy, and so relieved that we'll end this day on a high note. We'll all have a good time at the sing-along, and go home feeling great.

Except for me. I still can't help feeling wistful. If only Seb were here! It'll be hard to sing "We're All in This Together" without him. Miss Jenn isn't the only one who's had a disappointing day.

CHAPTER FORTY-FOUR

KOURTNEY

"Nini!" I grab her before she can scamper away again. She has been impossible to find all afternoon, and now we're staying for the sing-along, we *have* to get ready. Luckily Big Red and Ricky dug my makeup bag and our costumes out of the van. We're going to look good and sound even better. Or is that the other way around?

"I know, we need to change," she says. Ricky is lurking, too, both of them looking at me with their Bambi eyes. "But first we wanted to play something for you. It's a work in progress."

"We could play it to her on the van ride home," Ricky says to Nini.

"I know, but then everyone else would hear it as well, and it's supposed to be for Kourtney."

"Wait a minute!" I give them the *don't-walk* hand. "What are you guys talking about? What's supposed to be for me?"

"A song," Nini says, practically springy with excitement. "I wanted to write you a song, and Ricky and I have been working on it this afternoon."

"In *here*?" I'm incredulous. If Disneyland is the happiest place on earth, this convention may be the noisiest.

"We found a quiet corner," Ricky tells me, and Nini starts laughing.

"Remember what Mr. Mazzara said in class?" she asks me. "We did just what his collaborating scientists did. We imagined what isn't there, and then we stepped into the unknown."

"It was an empty room where a workshop had been canceled," says Ricky, more helpfully. "So, do you want to hear the song?"

Nini takes my arm. "We want to see what you think. It still needs work."

The empty room is nearby, so Ricky leads the way, holding his guitar case up as a shield so we can push through the crowds. I thought lots of people would have headed off by now, as we were planning to do, but clearly the sing-along is a bigger attraction than I realized. I'm so glad we've decided to stick around for it. Maybe it's

236

corny, but it's fun. And we all need some fun right now.

In the room Nini pulls me up a chair. She and Ricky stand in front of a whiteboard that reads *Workshop on Basketball Court Choreography Canceled Due to Instructor Injury.* Ouch. I hope they didn't injure themselves dancing on a basketball court somewhere. Way to give *HSM* a bad name.

"So," says Ricky, strumming his guitar, "the song was originally called 'Confusion.' But once Nini started working on it with me, we weren't confused anymore."

"It's about you and me, Kourt," Nini says, and I feel kind of emotional. It's been that kind of day. "And how . . . Well, you'll hear."

Ricky plays the opening chords, and Nini starts to sing.

> *When you're young, growing up sounds the perfect way*
> *To live your own life, decide which paths to take*
> *But turns out, it's harder to choose*
> *Just what will make you happy, make you win or lose*
>
> *That's why I need a friend like you*
> *That's why you're a dream come true*
> *That's why wherever we may roam*
> *Our friendship's the place we call home*

When there's a fork in the road, we're not sure what
    to do
Sometimes it's scary going somewhere new
We look to each other for a nudge along the way
And open our eyes to a brand-new day

That's why I need a friend like you
That's why you're a dream come true
That's why wherever we roam
Our friendship's the place we call home

Ricky joins in with a soft harmony on the chorus.
I'm crying, listening to them. They sound so good
together. *We* sound so good together. And I love what
Nini is saying here. Even though we might not be in the
same geographical location, we'll still be friends. Best
friends.

"You guys!" I say. "I'm really touched. That was
amazing."

"It still needs a little work," says Ricky, though he
looks pleased. "We'll practice it some more and maybe
work out a bridge when we're home. Right, Nini?"

She nods, still looking straight at me, tears glistening
in her eyes. *When we're home*, Ricky says. But how much

longer will Nini be at home in SLC? I'm going to miss her so much.

I'm careful not to say anything in front of Ricky. Nini hasn't told him anything yet—that much is pretty clear. The boy wouldn't be beaming like a fool in love if Nini had already dropped the knowledge on him.

"Maybe you could call the song 'Instructor Injury,'" I suggest, "as a tribute to this room where you wrote it, and I heard it."

"Or instead of 'Confusion' it could be 'Contusion,'" Ricky adds, and Nini points to the door.

"Okay, Ricky—Kourt and I are going to get changed in here. We'll see you at the sing-along. You probably won't recognize us, because we'll be so glamorous."

"Okay . . . but you're always glamorous," he says, brandishing his guitar case. Nini is already taking off her boots, because they really won't look good with her red Gabriella dress. "See you there."

While we get ready, it really hits me. When Nini moves to Denver for school, I am going to miss her every single day, and so will Ricky. What was I thinking, sending in that application to the Youth Actors Conservatory on her behalf? Way to go, Kourtney—always butting in and knowing best. Acting first and thinking later.

Selfish me would rather keep her at East High. But Nini has a special talent, and more people need to hear it and see it. She'll get the training and nurturing she needs in Denver. Then no one will be able to stand in her way.

"You really like the song, Kourt?" she asks me, shaking her hair loose from its ponytail.

"I love the way it's all about growing up and not growing apart," I say, and Nini beams at me. "Oh! I forgot to tell you. I met this cool girl named Carlota in my workshop today."

"And what? She's your new best friend?" Nini teases.

"Maybe she's yours," I tease back, and Nini looks mystified. "You won't believe this, but she goes to YAC in Denver. She's been there a year, and really loves it. I got her number so I could put you two in touch. You know, when the time is right."

Right for Nini, I think, *and wrong for me.*

"Thanks, Kourt!" Nini's face brightens. "It'll be good to know more people there."

"Well, I have *all* the connections," I say. "And all the eye shadow, so you better get over here."

So many changes are coming. Nini will make new

friends in Denver, of course. We'll have to get used to spending a lot of time apart. But that doesn't mean we'll lose the special thing we have.

I hope Nini's song is right.

CHAPTER FORTY-FIVE

Wrong about
the Sing-Along:

RICKY

The sing-along begins with "Start of Something New" but leaps to "Stick to the Status Quo." When I tell you that everyone in the Gabriella Montez Ballroom is going nuts, I am underselling it. We could all be movie extras in the cafeteria scene. There are girls in white knee socks and red shorts, and at least ten different versions of Sharpay wearing whatever it is that Sharpay wears. (They all hurt my eyes.) Some people are carrying fake copies of *Exploring American History* or wearing fake red mortarboards. Skater dudes in knit caps bounce around next to cheerleaders and kids in lab coats. The noise and energy are phenomenal, and Nini in her red dress? She takes my breath away.

It's weird singing "Get'cha Head in the Game" with two hundred other Troys, but for some reason, in all this crazy racket, my head clears. I was never a musicals kind of guy, as Carlos has pointed out several dozen times. I never really got what went on—onstage, backstage, any stage at all. Maybe I thought everyone who took part in "drama" was part of a clique, not real school. Not real life. And it was always something that Nini was doing, not me.

But here I am, singing louder than I ever thought possible, knowing every single word. I wheel out some of the stupid moves I came up with today in Golf Course Choreography, and some that Carlos taught us for the show. We're such theater kids—our group, every group. And here in this big noisy group, I feel like I belong.

I'm not sure I'd even tell Big Red this, but the sense of connection here is amazing. Who knew he'd be here as well, dancing in the aisle? (I mean, why did they even bother with chairs in this ballroom? They knew none of us would be sitting down.)

Nini dances up to me to sing "I Can't Take My Eyes Off of You" and I twirl her around until we're both dizzy. E.J. is two rows ahead, taking selfies with girls from random schools. I think about what he said this morning, when we were still out in the line—all that stuff about trusting your instincts. I would never tell him this, but it's pretty good advice.

Nini's song for Kourtney got me thinking. I've never written a song for my mom. Not ever. So for the holidays this year I'll write something special for her, and sing it via video chat or something so she knows I love her. "Wherever we may roam," as Nini sang, people are the ones who make us feel at home. So wherever my mom is working, or my dad is living, or I go to college, we'll never lose that feeling.

Not sure how I can get this into a song without it being too sappy. I'll try it out on Big Red, and if he gags or cries, I'll know it's too much.

Or maybe just right.

CHAPTER FORTY-SIX

Wrong about
the Sing-Along:

BIG RED

Sing-alongs are not my thing. Can we agree on that? I should not be here. I should be in the basement playing video games, or at Salt Lake Slices working. Instead I came here today like a baton in a relay race, passed from my mom's car to E.J.'s car, about to be passed to the school van for the return trip. There was no mention of a sing-along before I arrived. In fact, I'd had the impression that this was the last thing in the world everyone wanted to do.

But I'm here, and going with the flow. It's good to see Ricky enjoying himself, and not being tense and worried like he was this afternoon. He and Nini look really happy, singing every song at the top of their lungs. Whatever was wrong seems to be right. And whatever was right between me and Ashlyn now appears to be wrong.

Video games are much more straightforward. Opponents come at you, you strike back or jump out of the way. You climb levels and rack up high scores. If things go really bad, you start again. You can keep starting again every day of your life. In the virtual world, no one gets annoyed with you and leaves. (Or ignores your texts.)

But video games, I realize, are much less complicated than relationships with actual humans, especially female humans who go to East High School.

Ashlyn is hanging out with Gina farther down the row. Ashlyn is wearing her Ms. Darbus costume, and Gina is dressed as Taylor in scholastic-decathlon mode. They're trying out some of the silly dance moves they learned today in some class. They seem pretty much inseparable. Whenever I tried to talk to Ashlyn today, Gina was there, giving me the evil eye. I'm familiar with that look, because after Ricky and Nini broke up, Kourtney used it on a daily basis—not just with Ricky but with me.

It's not like I can text Ashlyn when she's just a few feet away. Maybe it'll be easier when we're back home.

I'm not saying that Ashlyn is acting cold or aloof toward me. On the way into the ballroom, she was friendly, asking me if I wanted to borrow parts of a costume from some of the other kids they'd met. But once our group found a spot, she and Gina moved away from me and Ricky. There's this awkwardness between us that I thought the sing-along might solve. If I could get a little closer to her, so we could sing together (though me not so much, as my talents really do lie elsewhere), maybe things would thaw.

So I start making my way down the row toward them. Everything is chaotic, and some chairs are lying on the ground, used as dangerous props during "Stick to the Status Quo." Miss Jenn and Carlos are so preoccupied with their Broadway-level choreography, I manage to wriggle past without them even noticing.

The song ends, and everyone is breathless, some people bent double. The emcee announces that by popular request the next song will be "Start of Something New" again, now that we're all warmed up. Ashlyn and Gina are right there, Ashlyn pulling off her Ms. Darbus necklace because, she tells Gina, it keeps getting caught in her hair.

I tap her on the shoulder. Now's my chance, in the lull between songs, to start a conversation. Get some of that sing-along magic floating my way.

So what do I say? What great line enters my head?

Nothing. I got nothing.

"Hey!" I finally manage to say. Ashlyn looks at Gina, and they both burst out laughing. "What?"

"It's just—that's all you ever say to me. In your texts."

"I'm a man of few words," I say, and Ashlyn smiles. "I only ever write texts to Ricky or sometimes my mom. They're never more than, like, one sentence."

"Maybe both of us are better in person," she says, and now I'm smiling as well. "I'm glad you got to come to the convention after all."

Any reply I might have, brilliant or otherwise, will have to wait. The next song has started, and the entire crowd is going wild.

CHAPTER FORTY-SEVEN

Miss Jenn's List of How She Was Wrong about the Sing-Along

1. Be honest. You didn't want to stay this late. Not having achieved so little. If E.J. hadn't brought this up, would you have suggested it? No. But look at everyone. They are SO happy. Resist the urge to text Mr. Mazzara in triumph. You can gloat in person next week at school.

2. Sing "Breaking Free" so loudly that you can barely speak afterward. Doesn't it feel good to celebrate the movie and its songs, rather than plotting to get a guest star and running yourself ragged?

3. Forget that this sing-along is packed with *HSM* superfans who know every frame of every movie, even the deleted scenes, until some kids you don't know tap your arm between songs and ask to take your picture—because they recognize you from the movie! Don't be coy when they ask you to re-create what they call the signature apple move (words + gesture + hit your mark + face toward the key light; it's not as simple as it looks, people!).

4. Don't be surprised when more kids gather wanting photos with you and (gulp!) your autograph. Sign your name so many times your hand hurts. Borrow a glitter pen off Kourtney; so much more dazzle! Try not to laugh out loud with sheer delight when the kids talk about posting your photo on Insta.

5. Tell everyone to come check out East High's spring production—whatever it ends up being. Because whether you have a guest star or not, you will put on the Best. Show. Ever.

6. Look around. Look at your students belting out numbers and dancing their hearts out. Look at the smiles on their faces and be proud of the role you play in their lives. You may not have achieved what you intended at the convention, but maybe you were wrong about everything. EVERYTHING. *This* is what's important for the kids, not your personal ambitions.

7. Remind yourself never to say any of the above to Mr. Mazzara. He's not the kind of guy who'll appreciate "Bop to the Top." Just the thought of Mr. Mazzara bopping makes you laugh uncontrollably. Reassure Carlos when he asks you if everything is okay. Remind yourself you're still in public. Sign some more autographs. Take some more pictures. Remember: All the world's a stage. *This could end up on Instagram.*

CHAPTER FORTY-EIGHT

Wrong about the Sing-Along:

CARLOS

The emcee announces there'll be just two more numbers in the sing-along, and everyone groans. How could the time fly so fast?

The first song, he says, will be the duet "What I've Been Looking For." When he announces this, the room goes wild—tcha! And then there's a pause for a technical glitch. Someone, he tells us, brought a therapy rodent to the convention and it's loose backstage.

We all look at Natalie.

"It's not me!" she protests. "Do you guys really think I'm the only person who has a therapy hamster?"

"How can there possibly be more than one of you in the world?" Gina asks, and Natalie looks offended.

"There's a whole online community, actually. And we prefer 'small friends' to 'rodents.'"

So on it goes, and I really hope that this doesn't mean an early end to the sing-along. This is the first time all day I've felt something approaching happiness. Of course, it's not perfect. But it's a spoonful of sugar at the end of hours of too much medicine. I just wish Seb was here to share it. (Too much sugar will rot my teeth.)

"Carlos." Now I'm hallucinating. Among all this racket of excited chatter, I think I can hear Seb's voice.

"Carlos." Someone touches my arm. I really must be tired, hearing things. Hearing people who aren't here. It's probably Big Red doing an impression. Or maybe it's the escaped therapy rodent, asking for help to hide.

I turn, ready to roll my eyes. But there, standing right beside me, is Seb! My mouth drops open. Is this really him? He's wearing a thick sweater and jeans, as though he's still at work on his family's farm. But can I see a trace of glitter in that lip gloss?

"Is it really you?" I ask him, and he smiles. "Did you teleport here or something? Tap your ruby slippers?"

"My brother is driving back to school in Missoula," Seb tells me. It really is him. He's really here! "He was leaving around noon, and he said he could drop me off here on his way north."

"But you didn't even know we'd still be here!" I can't believe that Seb has come all this way today. He had no idea we'd decided to stay late for the sing-along.

"I thought we'd get here earlier," he admits, pausing so Kourtney can smack welcome kisses on his cheeks. "We should have been here an hour ago, but some truck spilled oil on the interstate and we were held up. At the very least I thought I could arrive in time to ride back in the van with you all."

"That is so adorable!" I can't believe that Seb would come all the way here just to drive straight back again. "But insane. You do realize that, don't you? We could have left without you. We weren't planning on staying for the sing-along. It was just a last-minute decision."

"I wasn't worried." Seb shrugs, and gives his sweet smile again. It makes my heart skip a beat. "When you and I couldn't connect, I got in touch with E.J."

"E.J.?" This day gets stranger by the minute.

"He said he would stick around to drive me back to Salt Lake tonight, if I arrived too late and the van left without me."

Consider my mind blown. Seb and E.J. conspiring. Not just unexpected—unprecedented. Note to self: Hug E.J.—maybe at school on Monday, when he's washed his clothes clean of all that vegetable moss.

"I wanted to surprise you," Seb says, and now we're both laughing, holding each other's hands. "Surprise!"

We lean in close. "This is the best surprise ever," I tell him.

The emcee strolls back onstage with good news. The rodent is in a cage. The show can go on! And "What I've Been Looking For" is the perfect song to sing with Seb, and not just because he played Sharpay in our *HSM* production.

We sing the duet, along with the hundreds of other #HSMCon-goers in the room. But I think Seb's doing exactly the same thing I am, pretending we're the only people here.

We sing gazing into each other's faces, me taking the Ryan lines, and Seb reprising his brilliant Sharpay. All the misconnections of the weekend are forgotten. Here we are, together for the final duet, and for the "We're All in This Together" finale. (What did you think everyone would be singing? Come on!)

Two songs aren't much, but they're enough. Enough to remind me that Seb and I are perfect together.

CHAPTER FORTY-NINE

NINI

All good things must come to an end, as my grandmother always says, usually after she's just let me win at cards.

Once the sing-along is over, it really is time to go home. Miss Jenn promises we'll stop for burgers on the way, maybe once we're back in Utah, so if the van breaks down again we can be rescued by our families.

"Or Mr. Mazzara," Kourtney whispers to me. She's been humming the song Ricky and I wrote for her, which makes me happier than any workshop or master class.

Although Miss Jenn offered again to collect the van so we could all wait inside, we've insisted on walking together. It's cold—really, really cold—but not snowing or too icy underfoot. She wasn't kidding when she said she had to park a long way away. Also, Ricky tells me, the van was kind of in a snow drift, but hopefully it's melted. Or we can dig it out. We have Seb with us now, so there's an extra pair of hands.

"See you all at the rest stop," E.J. calls. Maybe he's planning on dropping by his other convention for a wordless farewell. Miss Jenn has made him promise to join us there for dinner, to break up the drive. Or tow the van.

I'm glad he's stopping there, too. Part of me wonders: Will this be the last time we're all together like this, and really happy? I know that sounds like a strange thing to think right after we've just had the most amazing time, singing with all these other amazing musical theater enthusiasts here at the convention. During the sing-along I was feeling even more excited to stretch my wings at the conservatory next semester. But I also realized that however cool it is, and however talented the people are there, there's no way they can ever replace the friends I have at East High.

Ricky walks with me through the lot, where cars and vans are streaming out into the night. Whenever the clouds part, we can glimpse a few stars, but the mountains are obscured by the darkness. He has his guitar case in one hand, and holds my right hand, his glove wrapping my mitten. I'm so pleased he liked his program. But all the signed programs in the world won't make next semester any easier.

"I wanted to tell you," he says, "that I've decided something."

This sounds ominous. "What?" I ask, trying not to seem too nervous.

"I realized that I was overthinking everything, about my mom and dad and the holidays. I just need to keep things simple right now."

"So you've decided?"

"Yeah. I'm going to stay with my dad over the holidays."

"Ricky!" I'm so happy. "So you can take part in the fundraising concert on Christmas Eve?"

"Sure can." We're both smiling, and practically dancing. It doesn't look strange because lots of other groups are making their way through the lot, all on a high from the sing-along. One group is even making a cheer pyramid. Where do they get the energy?

"That's the best news," I tell him. It's such a relief that he's come to this decision; I can see it on his face. He doesn't seem torn anymore.

"I guess I needed to be away from home to get some

perspective on it," says Ricky, swinging my hand. "For the first time I didn't feel pressure from anyone."

Kourtney has stopped to chat with a tall girl who's with an older woman. The girl is holding a YAC bag. This must be Carlota, the girl Kourtney met in her workshop today. I really want to go over, but what would I say to Ricky? What if he walked over with me? We're still holding hands. Eek.

I keep walking, almost dragging Ricky along. This is not the way I want him to find out about my secret plans.

But I can't resist glancing over my shoulder at Carlota and Kourtney.

"Who's Kourt talking to?" Ricky asks.

"I'm . . . um . . . not sure. A new friend." I'm stammering like a fool. "No. I mean—no one."

Ricky tugs on my hand to slow me down. "Hey," he says, his voice soft, and swirls me toward him. "Is everything okay?"

I want to tell him so bad. Right here and right now, under this big Wyoming winter sky, I really want to tell him. Keeping secrets from Ricky is awful.

"Yes," I say. Then I stop, mouth open like a fish. I do want to tell him about the opportunity in Denver, but I don't know what to say.

"There's the van!" Big Red shouts, and everyone else cheers. They're running down, racing to get out of the cold night. I hear laughter and bursts of singing. Everyone is so happy.

"Come on, people!" calls Miss Jenn. Ricky is still holding my hand, gazing into my eyes.

"What?" he asks, looking so worried. "You know you can tell me anything."

This is such a special moment. I can't spoil it with the truth. So I tell him something else—still true, but a different truth.

"I love you," I say. Ricky's face breaks into a smile.

"I love you, too," he replies, and starts to laugh.

"What's so funny?"

"Nothing. It's been a crazy trip, but everything's good now."

The van door slides open with a crash. Everyone is clambering in, shrieking about who sits where. Miss Jenn has started the engine.

"You're crazy," I whisper to Ricky, and give him the tightest hug, my eyes closed. The start of something new will have to wait. Nothing should spoil how happy we all are tonight.

"All right, then, let's hit the road," he says with the smile I love.

E.J. here. One last time before we drive back to the SLC.

This has been quite a weekend. Well, thirty-six hours, of which I spent about fifteen driving. But I've managed to squeeze in two different conventions and learned so much. Now is a time to reflect.

At my first convention, the one where I wasn't registered and had no business being, I learned about mindfulness and serenity. I learned that keeping quiet is sometimes better than jabbering. I learned that you need to double-check before turning on an industrial-strength blender. And I learned that living in the moment rather than obsessing about the past or worrying about the uncertainties of the future is the way to go.

As a result, I plan to be more chill next semester.

More mindful. I'm looking forward to the new year.

At my second convention, where I only got to spend this afternoon, I learned something very important as well. In the duet workshop I held Ricky's hands and looked into his eyes, while shouting the words of a song neither of us knew. A song that may or may not be an extra track in *High School Musical*. I suspect not.

From that experience I learned that not even someone with my theatrical experience can make a duet work with someone who's not feeling it.

Finally, a confession. I didn't want to make Miss Jenn feel bad, but something happened to me this afternoon after the duet class. I stayed late to talk with the teacher, then I managed to leave by the wrong door, the one that led to the valet parking area, where only teaching staff and "talent" were allowed to go.

You won't believe it, but this is how I managed to bump into Corbin Bleu on his way out of the convention! His driver was just there, and he was so cool about stopping to chat. We even got a photo together. He is a cool dude and such a good guy.

Corbin noticed the green stains on my clothes, and he totally agreed with me about the importance of drinking kale-and-broccoli smoothies. He says he drinks them all the time, and commended me on my nutritional knowledge. He also said that green really suits me.

So that was my weekend. I'm so glad I let myself get lost.

E.J. out.

3000 likes

Add a comment...

ACKNOWLEDGMENTS

Many, many thanks to the amazing *High School Musical: The Musical: The Series* team, especially my dear friend Tim Federle. Thank you, Tim, for creating an incredible show and making my kid think I'm "cool" again. Thank you to all the folks at Disney, especially my amazing editor Brittany Rubiano and Disney Channel's Miriam Ogawa, who let me keep my favorite line.

Thanks always to Mouse Team Mel: my darlings Emily Meehan, Kieran Viola, Jocelyn Davies, Seale Ballenger, Elke Villa, Holly Nagel, Joann Hill, and Marci Senders. Thanks to my agents Richard Abate, Martha Stevens, and Ellen Goldsmith-Vein.

Thanks to my huge support network of family and friends, especially my DLC fam, the beloveds text thread, and my CH peeps.

Thanks to Mike and Mattie, always.